I Love You
By Brian Bowman

I0542834

BLACK JACK

ENTERTAINMENT

For more information or to order more books please contact:

Black Jack Entertainment Agency LLC.

1046 Geers

Columbus, Ohio 43206

(614) 364-1816

bowman_brian@att.net

ISBN: 978-0-9845233-1-3

BLACK JACK ENTERTAINMENT AGENCY LLC
COLUMBUS, OHIO 43206

PRINTED IN THE UNITED STATES OF AMERICA

First and foremost I would like to give all of the credit to GOD for making the production of this book possible. With Him all things are possible. This book is dedicated to my entire family (biological and extended). I would not be able to achieve any of my goals without your support. I would also like to thank all of the people that support me whom I haven't had the pleasure of meeting. Last but not least, I would like to thank the entire staff of BLACK JACK ENTERTAINMENT AGENCY LLC for helping this dream become a reality.

Chapter 1

Slices of sunlight fought through the gaps of the closed drapes while a couple by the name of David and Felicia desperately tried to combine their souls. The lovemaking between the two newlyweds was as intense as a fight between two pit bulls. The passion they shared was unexplainable.

"Don't stop! Don't stop, daddy," Felicia yelled as she dug her nails into David's back.

"I promise I'll never stop," David replied, while inserting himself deeper into Felicia.

As the tall brown-skinned woman wrapped her legs around David's gravitating hips, she began to climax.

"Ooooohhh! That's it, baby. That's it."

"Daddy's cumming with you," David yelled as he exploded inside of his wife.

Sweat dripped into Felicia's eyes as she stared up at her muscular husband. Even though the two had been an item since the sixth grade and married for eight months, the extent of her love for David still blew her mind. There was nothing she would not do for him, and this he knew. David would often use Felicia's love for him to manipulate her. His love for her was just as strong, but his selfishness and love for himself were stronger.

"Do you want any breakfast?" Felicia asked while walking into the bathroom and starting the shower.

"We don't have time," David replied, joining Felicia in the shower. "You know Chris usually leaves around eleven o'clock every morning. We've got to get there before he leaves."

Felicia was hoping that David had changed his mind about going to see Chris.

"I don't know if I can go through with this," she said in a frightened voice.

"You don't have a choice!" David yelled.

"Why don't you just get past this bullshit?" Felicia yelled back, stepping out of the shower.

"I'll get past this bullshit once it's finished, and you know I can't move forward without your help. Now are you with me or not?"

"You said we were finished after the last one!" she cried, with tears streaming down her face. "There's no way I can do it again. I haven't had a good night's sleep since all this bullshit started. You know all this is against my beliefs. Please, baby, don't make me do this again. Pleeease!"

"I know I said we were finished, baby, and we almost are. Just a few more, and this whole nightmare will be over. I need you, baby. I can't do this without you."

Felicia was at a crossroads. Once again she was being forced to compromise her life, freedom, and religion for the man she loved. The man she married. She really didn't know which was worse, the horrible things she had to do or the fact of David making her do them.

"I don't think I can do this again," Felicia said as she exited the bathroom.

David followed his wife into the bedroom and said, "If you loved me then you would do this."

That one sentence was all the convincing that Felicia needed. She put on her clothes, lit the half cigarette that was in the ashtray, and headed out of the motel en route to Chris's home.

Chapter 2

Detective Michael Mathews pulled in back of the many police cruisers that were parked in front of the home of DeJuan Anderson. His body had been discovered by his girlfriend late last night.

"This is the weirdest shit I've ever seen," said the young police officer as he walked over to the detective. "We found at least two hundred thousand dollars under the victim's bed. Whoever mutilated him must not have needed the money, because they sure didn't take it."

"Make sure nobody touches a goddamn thing in there until I'm finished. And get these motherfuckin' news cameras the hell out of here. I don't want any names — or other information, for that matter — released, do you hear me?" the detective yelled while lighting a cigar.

"Yes, sir!" the police officer replied.

Detective Mathews wanted to go over DeJuan's house with a fine tooth comb. He knew that the victim was powerful both physically and financially. For someone to come into this man's home meant a war in the making. DeJuan had a long list of friends that would be hell-bent on revenge, which meant the quieter they could keep this thing, the better.

"Somebody finally got old D," said Michael's partner,

Brian. "They fucked him up pretty bad, too."

"Any leads on who might have had the balls to off one of the dreaded YBEs?" Detective Mathews asked.

"Yeah — another YBE!" Brian answered.

Daniel Washington, leader of the Young Black Entrepreneurs — which happened to be the most feared group in Columbus — stood in his living room yelling at the top of his lungs.

"I want the motherfucker that did this dead by night-fall! Do you bastards understand? If I don't hear about a motherfucker getting his head cut off on the eleven o'clock news then I'm going to personally kill each and every one of you."

"Calm down, bra," said Tony, one of Daniel's top lieutenants. "All those threats ain't necessary. Besides, we don't have a clue as to who the hell did this to DeJuan."

Tony had been feeling very irritated at Daniel's attitude lately. Although the two had known each other since the first grade and started the YBE together, Tony was being treated unfairly. He was very aware of the way he was being treated and had begun to get fed up. The length of their friendship was the only thing keeping the short-tempered man and anyone else from killing Daniel. He and his brother Chris had saved Daniel's life numerous times in the past.

"Well, I suggest you find out who did this and handle

it — LIEUTENANT!" Daniel said sarcastically. "Where the hell is Chris? Somebody get that lazy motherfucker on the phone," he demanded.

"I've been trying all day. He's probably broken up about DeJuan and drowning his sorrow in a Hennessy bottle. I'm going over to his house as soon as I leave here."

"Please do, and call me as soon as you get there."

Chapter 3

David sat across from Felicia in the run-down diner, trying to calm her nerves. Tears poured down her face and fell into the plate of cold pancakes and eggs that sat in front of her.

"Baby, eat your food. It's getting cold."

"I don't want this shit! I don't want nothing but for you to leave me the hell alone," Felicia yelled.

"Calm down, Boo," David said in a low tone. "We don't need to draw any attention to us. Now I need you to get yourself together so we can finish this shit."

"This shit is finished! It's finished for me, anyway. I tried to help you, David, but I just can't do this anymore," the hysterical woman screamed with tears running down her face.

Everyone in the diner turned to look at Felicia.

"You're making a fucking scene!" David said in a low but stern tone. "Now I'm really getting sick and fuckin' tired of having to go through this shit with you. I've been taking care of your stankin' ass since the fucking sixth grade! Now that I need you to do something for me, it's a goddamn problem. Well, fuck that! If your ungrateful ass is just gonna leave me out here stuck, knowing that I can't move forward without you, then that means you never loved me in the first place."

"I can't believe you can sit over there and say those things to me. I've put up with all of your drug deals, police chases, swat raids, shoot outs, and hood rat bitches for almost twelve years — and this is how you talk to me? Do you have any idea of the things that I've been through in the last couple of days?"

The waitress and the cook, along with everyone else in the diner, all had their attention on Felicia now.

"Maybe I should call the police or something," said the short, round-faced cook with a large spoon in his hand.

"I think she is having a breakdown or something," the waitress replied.

"Well, she needs to have it somewhere else. That bitch is running off the customers," the cook said angrily.

"Oh, please. We hardly had any customers in the first place. Besides, in this neighborhood I doubt very seriously if anybody's gonna be offended by a woman venting her problems. She's probably just trying to clear her head and get things off of her chest," the waitress said in a sympathetic voice while walking over to the table. "Would you like some more coffee or anything else, sweetheart?"

"No, thank you. We're fine. Just give me the check and we'll be leaving," Felicia replied.

After receiving payment for the bill plus her tip, the waitress watched Felicia walk out of the diner. She turned around and said to the cook, "You were right. That bitch is crazy."

Tony walked down the hall of the apartment building until he reached his brother's house. He had been trying to contact him all night and was beginning to worry.

"This nigga is probably laid up in here with some ho. I could be fucking dead and this bastard won't even answer the phone."

As Tony attempted to knock on the door, it swung open. He pulled his 357 from his waistband and called out to his brother frantically.

"Chris! Chris! Are you in here?"

Tony had a horrible feeling in the pit of his stomach. As he slowly crept through the door with pistol in hand, his fears were confirmed. Chris lay in the middle of the living room floor with three bullet holes in his head. Filled with emotions, Tony searched the rest of the apartment, then fell to his knees beside his brother.

"Nooooo, bra! Who in the hell did this? Wake up, bra! Talk to me," Tony yelled knowing that would be impossible.

After gaining his composure, Tony decided to look around the apartment for clues. After finding nothing, he pulled out his cell phone and called Daniel to deliver the news.

"Someone shot him in his fucking face three times,"

Tony cried into the phone.

"Do you have any idea of who could have done this?"

"If I knew who did this shit, I would be over there with my pistol stuck up that motherfucker's ass," Tony said angrily.

"Damn! First DeJuan and now Chris. Somebody is trying to start a war with me. Well, the son of a bitch is not going to get away with this," Daniel yelled. "They don't know who the hell they are fucking with! I'll bet it was that punk ass Mook. He has been hating on me for years. Well, if it's war he wants, then its war he's got. That bastard is gonna feel the wrath of the YBE," he said with an evil look on his face.

Daniel's ranting and raving was starting to annoy Tony. It seemed that he had taken the death of Tony's brother and made it into another personal event for him to boast about his status and how everyone envied him.

"Are you out of your fucking mind?" Tony interrupted. "My motherfuckin' brother is dead, and you talking about some nigga hating on you. This shit ain't about your punk ass. It's about whoever killed my brother and that motherfucker paying. Fuck you and the YBE!"

"Calm down, Tony. I know you are upset, and that's why I'm gonna let you get away with talking to me crazy. Now what you need to do is get the hell out of that apartment before the police show up, and get over here so we can handle this," Daniel said.

Although Tony wanted to continue to vent his anger, he knew Daniel was right. He hung up the phone, said his last goodbyes to his brother, and left the apartment. While driving, all of Tony's thoughts were about Chris. The two were only one year apart and had always been extremely close. Suddenly he had a vision of DeJuan.

Maybe the two murders are connected, he thought to himself. *But why, and who's next?*

As Tony pulled into Daniel's driveway, he was hesitant about getting out. There was something strange about all of this and he couldn't help but feel that Daniel was somehow responsible. Especially after the situation that took place with David. From that point on it was a proven fact that Daniel could not be trusted and was now Tony's prime suspect in his brother's murder. He knew that Daniel was not the actual trigger man. There was no way he could have stood up against Chris in a fight. But Tony was sure that he had some type of involvement and was determined to settle this tonight. Tony counted the bullets in his gun and walked up the driveway toward the door.

I swear if this motherfucker gives me one indication of his involvement, I'm gonna blow the back of his head up against a wall, Tony thought as he knocked on Daniel's door.

Chapter 4

Rain began to fall from the sky as David and Felicia stood in the parking lot of GJ's Lounge, going over their plans.

"OK, baby! This is it. Now don't worry, I'm right behind you. Put the gun in the front of your pants like I showed you. The doorman is only gonna look inside of your purse. Little Ronnie usually sits all the way in the back. All you got to do is get him out here to his car and I'll handle the rest," David said in a convincing voice.

"And just how the hell do you think I'm supposed to get him outside?" Felicia asked while trying to hold back her frustrations with David.

"I don't know! Shit, offer the nigga a blow job, show him one of your titties, grab his dick or something. Use that big ass head of yours and come up with an idea."

"I see now that your respect for me has completely gone down the drain. I'm your fucking wife, David," Felicia screamed as tears mixed with raindrops ran down her face. "You want me to go offer this nigga a blow job? You want me to get this nigga to his car by any means necessary, huh? I got you," Felicia said while wiping the tears from her face.

"Baby, don't go in there all emotional and fuck this up. Get your motherfuckin' head right!" David demanded.

"Don't start worrying about my emotions now, motherfucker! I got my head right. Now I'm about to go get Little Ronnie's head right," the angry woman said as she walked toward the front door of the bar.

"Don't play with me, bitch!" David yelled as he watched his wife swing her hips through the door and past the doorman.

GJ's Lounge was unusually crowed for a Thursday night. The bar was filled with the smell of smoke and liquor. Felicia's eyes searched the entire bar until she finally spotted Little Ronnie sitting in the corner booth entertaining two young ladies. The emotional woman needed a drink to calm her nerves. She fought her way to the bar and ordered two double shots of Hennessy on the rocks. After taking a giant swallow from one of the glasses, she headed to the booth where Little Ronnie was sitting.

"Quite the ladies' man, aren't you?" Felicia said as she offered the second glass to Little Ronnie.

"Hey girl! Long time, no see," the husky man responded while standing up to give Felicia a hug. "Thanks for the drink."

"Anytime, honey. Are you going to offer me a seat?"

"Sure! Sure! You ladies are going to have to excuse use for a while. I need to holla at Miss Lady for a minute," Little Ronnie said while looking directly at Felicia.

The two women reluctantly got up from the booth and brushed past Felicia while rolling their eyes at her.

"So, to what do I owe the pleasure of this visit?" Little Ronnie asked.

"I really don't know," Felicia responded. "For some strange reason you have been on my mind almost every day. So I figured I would come up here and buy you a drink, and hopefully you can tell me how you have invaded my thoughts."

Little Ronnie was surprised by what he was hearing. Felicia had always been devoted to David. Even though she had been the leading lady in a number of his wet dreams, Ronnie had long ago cast out the possibility of any type of intimacy between the two. Especially after what had happened to her and her husband. Now she was sitting next to him with no David to worry about.

"I'm sure as the night goes on and the drinks continue, we can figure out the cause of this invasion," Ronnie said with a perverted look in his eyes.

"A few more drinks may cause another type of invasion," Felicia said seductively.

"Well, I'll drink to that!" the horny man said, signaling the barmaid over to his table.

Felicia was beginning to feel guilty. She had never even come close to being with anyone other than David. Although the thought of it made her sick to her stomach, she couldn't help the attraction she had for Little Ronnie. She had always found the man attractive and couldn't help but notice the way he would sneak a look at her whenever

David wasn't watching. As she finished her drink the bar-maid set another in front of her. The woman's heart began to throb as she felt Little Ronnie's hand rubbing her thigh. A feeling of rage began to take over the moistness between her legs, as she thought of David standing outside waiting for the two to come out. The way she had been treated by her husband lately was really bothering her. The awful things that David had made her do in the past couple of days had begun to wear on her sanity.

I thought David was different from other men. Next he'll probably ask me to sell my pussy for his cigarette money. And this fat motherfucker was supposed to have been David's friend, Felicia thought to herself. "Your feelings for David are not going to get in the way of tonight?" she asked in a low tone.

Ronnie was really confused now. Either Felicia did not remember what had happened, or she was trying to set him up. Or maybe she knew about David all along and under-stood that what happened was just business.

"Hell, no!" Ronnie responded. "I wouldn't let a hur-ricane get in the way of me and you tonight. Besides, David is finished. It's time you get over that motherfucker and get with a real nigga."

Ronnie's response only enraged Felicia more. The an-ger she felt gave her the courage to carry out the plan. She leaned over and kissed Little Ronnie passionately while rubbing his penis.

"I think you should consider changing your name to

Big Ronnie," Felicia said while biting the man's bottom lip. "Come on. Let's get out of here."

Meanwhile David stood outside, a nervous wreck. He knew that the remarks he had just made to his wife were a little extreme. Even though his wife's feelings were hurt, tonight's mission was more important. Not knowing what was going on inside the bar finally got the best of him. David walked into GJ's Lounge somehow unnoticed by the doorman. It didn't take him long to spot Felicia and Little Ronnie. The sight of his wife almost in another man's lap sent a chill up his spine. The thought of killing Ronnie and the obedience of his wife were a substitution for his feelings of jealousy and betrayal. As Ronnie stood up and Felicia grabbed her purse, David knew they were headed outside. With no concern about being seen by the two, David headed back to the parking lot. Before exiting the bar, he took one last glance at Little Ronnie's hand all over his wife's ass.

I'm going to enjoy making this motherfucker die slow! David thought to himself, lighting a cigarette.

Meanwhile Little Ronnie was all smiles as he walked out of GJ's Lounge arm in arm with the great David Taylor's wife. In his opinion he had accomplished the unaccomplishable and defeated the undefeatable. The beautiful woman at his side was only the spoils of war. Felicia, on the other hand, had plans of her own. She was going to kill two birds with one stone. She had every intention of making David sorry for treating her the way he had. The original plan was still in effect, but Felicia was going to show Little Ronnie the time of his life first. She knew David would be watching and hopefully realize what he was in jeopardy of losing.

"Where did you park, daddy?" Felicia asked.

"Over in the corner by the alley, baby. Don't you see the Heavy Chevy over there?"

"I see you, Boo. That motherfucker is big enough for me to put this thang on you right here," Felicia purred.

"Damn! You are a frisky little motherfucker, aren't you? Well, I'm like Janet Jackson, baby. *Anytime and anyplace*," Ronnie sang as he opened the door to his truck.

Upon entering the truck, Felicia didn't waste any time. She hopped right into Little Ronnie's lap and pushed her tongue down his throat. The pistol that was in her pants began to poke her in the pelvis. She did not want to risk Ronnie feeling the gun pressed against him.

"You are in for a special treat," Felicia said as she climbed off of Ronnie's lap and started to unzip his pants.

David tiptoed to the rear of Little Ronnie's truck without being noticed. His plan was working out perfectly. He eased his way along the side of the truck to the driver's side window only to receive the shock of his life: the love of his life licking the testicles of Little Ronnie.

"What the fuck are you doing?" David screamed in a rage.

Upon hearing David's voice, Felicia bit down on

Ronnie's penis as hard as she could. Blood mixed with urine exploded from the sides of her mouth as Ronnie screamed in excruciating pain. While attempting to break the pit bull type lock the crazed woman had on his penis, Ronnie discovered the pistol hanging from Felicia's pants. David realized Ronnie's intentions even before Ronnie himself, and moved quickly. He reached through the window and dug directly into both of Ronnie's eye sockets with his thumb and index finger. The pain Ronnie was feeling was unbearable. Although amazed that a person as small and fragile as Felicia would be the one to take him out, he knew his life was just seconds from ending. The fear of being seen or heard by the drunken bar crowd was no longer a factor as the screams of the hurting man caused a rage inside Felicia's head. She pulled the gun from her waistband and placed it underneath Ronnie's chin.

"Kill that motherfucker," David growled with a sinister grin on his face.

Although upset with David, the thought of being able to please her man filled Felicia's mind as she fired four shots into Ronnie's head. With blood all over her face she rose up and spit out a huge portion of the penis she had just chewed off of the eyeless, brainless corpse that belonged to Little Ronnie. The savage act committed by his wife made David feel like a proud father. He had created the plan and his partner had carried it out perfectly. His mind was filled with the joy of revenge.

The bloodied couple fled the scene without being noticed. As the club let out at 2:15 a.m., Ronnie's body was
discovered.

Chapter 5

Tony pushed one of the two bodyguards who attempted to search him as he entered the home of Daniel Washington.

"Get your goddamn hands off of me!" he yelled while withdrawing his pistol.

"I don't know why you two idiots keep trying Tony. One day he's gonna fuck around and blow both of your heads off," Daniel said as he entered the room with a bottle of Hennessy and two glasses in his hands. "Come on in and have a seat, bra."

Tony walked over to the couch with pistol still in hand. Daniel concentrated on not showing how nervous he was, while pouring their drinks. In an attempt to break the ice, he poured close to a fourth of the liquor on the floor.

"For DeJuan and Chris," Daniel said in a sad voice.

"Save all the rituals," Tony snapped. "I wanna know who in the fuck killed my brother and why."

"Like I told you on the phone, I think it was that motherfuckin' Mook. He's trying to get our attention. You are my bulldozer and he knows this. By killing Chris he can get your head all fucked up where you won't be thinking straight. He's counting on you coming straight at him with no plan, just raw emotion. We gotta put both of our heads together on this one, baby!"

Although Tony hated to admit it to himself, Daniel was beginning to make a lot of sense. Mook had always been known to be diabolical. By hitting the key players of the YBE, the city would belong to him in no time. On the other hand, Daniel had always had it out for Mook. Could he be setting all this up in order to have an excuse to go to war with Mook? Tony did not trust Daniel any more than he did two hours ago, but realized he was going to need his help to get to the bottom of his brother's murder.

"So what do you suggest we do?" Tony asked with tears in his eyes.

"I already put a tail on his black ass and I got a couple of niggas in every club in the city. You know how fast shit travels in the streets. If that arrogant bastard had anything to do with either one of the murders he is gonna brag. As soon as he does, I'll send word to have his mother's head cut off!"

"Well, let's say for a minute that it wasn't Mook. Who else would want Chris dead?" Tony asked with an extremely serious look on his face.

"Every broke ass nigga in the city of Columbus!" Daniel yelled. "Now I know you are upset, but you gotta get your head together and understand that this was not a personal hit on Chris but a blow to the YBE, and there's no telling who is going to be next."

The two men were interrupted by the bodyguard handing Daniel the telephone.

"Yeah!" he yelled into the receiver. "What? You bullshit-tin'! Fuck! Don't you bring your motherfuckin' ass back here until you've found out who in the hell did this shit. UNDERSTAND?" Daniel demanded while slamming the phone.

"What happened?" Tony asked with a puzzled on his face.

"The motherfucker got Little Ronnie. Now do you believe that this is not a personal beef, but a fuckin' take-over attempt?" Daniel yelled, throwing his half full glass of Hennessy against the wall.

Tony realized that Daniel was right, but that did not change the fact that he was somehow responsible his broth-er's death, no matter how inadvertently.

"All right boss, tell me what you want me to do."

"Not this time, buddy. I want that fucking Mook to look me right in the eye and know the cause of his destruc-tion," Daniel said with a sinister grin on his face.

"That's all well and good, but I get to pull the fucking trigger," Tony replied while grabbing his boss's arm.

"You got that coming, bra," Daniel answered as he turned and hugged Tony's neck.

The two men, along with twelve other bodyguards, left Daniel's home, headed for Mook's residence.

Mook poured two glasses of Moët and handed one to the young lady sitting on his couch. The thirty-one-year-old dark-skinned man was well known throughout the strip clubs for his x-rated after parties. At times he would take up to four girls home and explore every kinky fantasy his imagination would allow. The girls would be well compensated for their actions with enough blow and ecstasy pills to erase any type of morals they thought they had. This was Mook's only way of dealing with the fact that no matter how much money he made, he would never have the power or respect of Daniel or anybody else in the YBE. His jealousy for Daniel over the years had grown into an obsession that prevented him from enjoying his own success. The attention that he got from strippers and any other females who were willing to be paid for sexual favors was the only thing that took his mind off his competition. The reality of knowing that he could never beat the YBE and become the king of the streets made his drug and sex habits that much worse.

"Here you go, sweetheart," Mook said as he handed the glass of champagne to the well-built lady. "What did you say your name was again?"

"Angie!" the woman answered in an upset voice. "How the hell can you bring a woman into your house and not even know her name?"

"Hell, I don't need to know your name. Unless what you got makes me want to come back for seconds."

"Trust me, you'll be back!" Angie said as she stood up over Mook, lifted her leg into the air, and rested her ankle on his shoulder. "Do you think you can handle all that?"

"I guess we are about to find out," Mook said as he lifted the woman in the air with both of her legs resting on his shoulders, while placing his tongue inside her.

Mook carried the woman up the stairs and into one of the huge bedrooms. He threw her onto the bed and began to rip his clothes off all in one motion. While attempting to climb on top of the woman, she pushed him on his back and began to ride him.

"Goddamn! You were right. I am gonna have to come back for seconds," Mook moaned as he enjoyed his trick for the night.

"I told you, motherfucker. By the time I'm through with —"

The sight of fourteen armed men standing in the bedroom interrupted the woman's gloating. Before she could scream or attempt to warn Mook, the bullet from Daniel's .45 entered into her skull.

Chapter 6

"What the hell is going on, Mike?" Brian asked the detective in a confused voice as they stood in the parking lot of GJ's Lounge. "This is the second YBE member killed in less than a week. And who in the fuck would be sick enough to bite Ronnie's dick off?"

"The answer to that question should be revealed as soon as the DNA sample of all that blood comes back from the lab tomorrow. There has got to be some saliva, hair, or something in that truck belonging to the killer."

"That still does not explain what is going on," Brian said with a sad look on his face.

"War! That's what the hell is going on. The streets have a sick version of recycling. Old DeJuan and Little Ronnie here are gone, but you can best believe their replacements will be three times worse. The streets have been recycling niggas long before me and you, and will continue to long after me and you are gone," Detective Mathews yelled.

"So we are out here trying to make the streets better for the fuck of it, huh? According to you, there is no hope. Why did you even sign up for law enforcement if this is how you feel?" Brian asked his partner.

"My probation officer made me! Now get your sentimental ass over here and dust the truck for fingerprints," the detective demanded.

Detective Mathews grew up in the streets of Columbus, Ohio and attended school with the majority of the members of the YBE. Michael Mathews was once a member of the YBE himself, but after witnessing his mother lose everything from her crack addiction, he wanted nothing to do with the illegal organization. He vowed that every drug dealer would pay for the pain and humiliation of his mother. Michael would find all of Daniel's drug houses and throw cocktail firebombs through the windows. As the workers would run out of the burning houses, Michael would beat the hell out of them with his baseball bat. His vigilante efforts got the attention of the YBE in short time and Daniel had Michael kidnapped. Chris and David beat him half to death while Daniel watched and laughed. The men were interrupted by DeJuan dragging Michael's mother into the room screaming and kicking. Daniel gave Ms. Mathews the choice of picking her half dead son up off the floor and leaving with him, or performing oral sex on every male in the room including her son for twenty dollars' worth of crack. Michael lay on the floor half conscious and watched his mother perform oral sex on every man in the room. David and Chris pulled Michael off the floor and removed his pants. As Ms. Mathews crawled toward her son in an attempt to finish her part of the deal, Tony burst into the room and demanded that the two be set free. That was the last Michael ever saw of his mother or any type of compassion from himself ever again. He joined the police force a year later and promised he would take down the YBE.

"The people from inside the bar all confirm that Ronnie left with a female," a young officer walked over to Michael and said.

"Do we have a name?"

"Felicia Taylor."

"Are you sure?" Michael questioned.

"Everyone in the bar has the same story, sir," the officer answered.

Brian could not help but notice the look of shock on the detective's face.

"Do you know her?" he asked.

"Yeah. She is my cousin. I haven't seen her since she married that punk David. I need for you to find both Chris and Tony and bring them in for questioning," the detective ordered.

"I'm on it right now," Brian responded while rushing to his car.

Detective Mathews knew that if anyone knew what was going on with Felicia, it would be Tony and Chris. The two of them had always looked at David as a brother and probably felt obligated to take care of Felicia after what Daniel did to her husband. If she had any type of involvement in Ronnie's murder, those two were at the bottom of it. Michael's thoughts were interrupted by the ringing of his cell phone.

"Detective Mathews speaking."

"Yeah it's me, Brian. I guess Chris won't be able to answer any questions."

"And why the hell not?" the detective yelled.

"Because he's dead."

"Fuck! Stay right there. We're on the way — and don't touch shit until I get there," he ordered while hanging up the phone.

Chapter 7

"This is a lovely house you have here, Mook," Daniel said in a sarcastic voice.

"What the fuck is going on here?" Mook yelled as he wiped the brain fragments from his face.

"Time to pay the piper. You've been a very naughty boy. Did you actually think that you would win a war against the YBE? We own Columbus and everyone in it. Every dollar you make is because I allow it! Every whore you fuck is because I allow it! The only reason that your sorry ass mother did not have an abortion when pregnant with you is because I didn't allow it. And this is the way you repay me, by killing my top dogs!"

"I ain't killed no motherfuckin' body!" Mook yelled while jumping up off of the bed.

With incredible speed Tony leaped across the room and smacked Mook with his pistol. He continued to beat him until the weapon he was holding broke into two pieces.

"You killed my brother, motherfucker. Now you're gonna die slow."

Mook could tell by the tears in Tony's eyes and the rage in his voice that he felt that he was Chris's killer.

"I swear on my kid's life that I had nothing to do with your brother. I didn't even know that he was dead," Mook moaned with whatever little bit of energy he had left.

"Bullshit!" Daniel yelled. "It really does not matter now if you tell the truth or not. Either way it goes, you are one dead motherfucker," he growled as he instructed one of the henchmen with him to open the top of a gas can he was holding. "Tony, would you like to do the honors?"

Even though Tony had a gut feeling that Mook was innocent of his brother's murder, rage got the better of him. He snatched the gas can and doused Mook with the flammable liquid.

"I'll see all you bastards in hell!" Mook managed to stutter out while choking on the gas that covered him.

"Hell won't even be big enough for the two of us," Daniel responded as Tony thumped a lit cigarette on the bloody man lying in front of him.

Instantly Mook's body burst into flames. His screams echoed off of the walls while the YBE stood and watched their arch rival's demise. Tony's thirst for revenge still was not quenched, though. He knew deep down inside that he had just murdered an innocent man. The fact that Mook had always been a thorn in the side of the YBE eased Tony's guilt a bit, but the need to find his brother's killer still existed. As the men exited the home that belonged to the burning corpse, Daniel stopped and put his arm around Tony's shoulder.

"That was a pretty nice piece of ass old Mook had with him, huh?" Daniel asked with a devilish grin.

"Keep the jokes," Tony responded as he pulled away from Daniel.

Detective Mathews shook his head as he looked down at the body of Christopher Dennis. The two had gone back since the sixth grade. Although he had grown to hate the man, he felt a certain sadness come over him. It was not a feeling of sorrow for the death of a friend, but the fact that Chris and DeJuan did not die by his hands like he vowed they would. His thoughts were interrupted by the sight of his partner Brian standing in the corner, whispering on his cell phone. His distrust of everyone, including his partner, made him wonder just who it was on the other end of that cell phone. Brian was always an upfront and honest type of guy. He was too clumsy to be secretive. This was exactly the reason that Michael never trusted him. To him the whole Barney Fife thing was just an act. His instincts told him that Brian was laying it on extra thick in an attempt to mislead him. Either he was an undercover for internal affairs, or crooked as a question mark. Whichever it was, Detective Mathews was on to him.

"The little lady worried about you?" he asked while walking toward Brian.

"Yeah, she usually expects me home around midnight. Anytime after that she swears some punk has offed me in an alley," Brian responded while quickly hanging up the phone with a worried look on his face.

"I'll finish up here. Go home to the wife. We don't want her getting any bags under those pretty little eyes of hers."

Brian did not know whether to take that statement as a compliment or a blatant flirt. His feathers were ruffled and that was exactly what Detective Mathews wanted to do.

"I'm cool. Besides I don't want to fall behind in the investigation. Did they tell you that Tony was seen leaving here last night?" Brian asked.

"Yeah, and by the stage of rigor mortis and the amount of decomposition, I would say that old Chris here has been dead for about two days, which means Tony already knows."

"So what's next?" Brian asked with a puzzled look on his face.

"We sit back and watch the fireworks. Tony is going to go on a killing spree until he gets the motherfucker that did his brother. All we have to do is sit back and let him find our killer for us," Detective Mathews said as he lit a cigarette. "He'll kill off the majority of the little bastards on the streets, and we arrest him in the end for all their murders. Two birds with one stone and a lot less paperwork."

"That is the sickest fucking plan that you have had yet. You know what? I think I will take you up on that offer and call it a night. I suggest you do the same, because that warped ass brain of yours needs a rest!" Brian said in an angry voice.

"It takes a warped brain to outsmart a sneaky little

fucker like you," Detective Mathews said under his breath as he watched his partner walk away.

Brian called Daniel as soon as he reached his car and told him exactly what Detective Mathews had planned.

"Outside of the screams of that bitch ass nigga Mook, that's the second best thing that I've heard all night. That fucking Tony has become unmanageable anyway. We'll let the clever little detective handle him. I need for you to find David's wife Felicia and bring her to me. Some people at the club said they saw her with Little Ronnie. And try to make sure Michael doesn't catch on to your stupid ass," Daniel ordered.

"Please! I've got that dumb bastard thinking exactly what I want him to. He's too stupid to catch on to me," Brian gloated.

"Trust me, that man is far from stupid, and if he is on to you, your country ass would never know it. Just do exactly what I tell you to and nothing else," Daniel demanded.

"Yeah but I think—"

"That's just it, motherfucker! I don't pay you to think!" Daniel interrupted. "If you were good at thinking then I would be working for you instead of you for me. Now do what the fuck I tell you to. No more, no less."

Detective Mathews stood in the window looking down at the car of his partner. The high frequency bug that he placed inside his partner's car on the way upstairs let him know exactly who Brian was talking to this time. He'd always had a hunch that Brian was working for Daniel. He also knew that once the seed was planted in Daniel's head, his plan would unfold. Now all he had to do was let Tony find out that Daniel planned on setting him up for the fall, and then watch as the mighty empire crumbled. His cousin Felicia was the perfect person to deliver this news to Tony. Finding her before the rest of the police force did was his only problem. He still hadn't figured out just who was pulling her strings and why they would use her. He couldn't imagine her killing anybody, especially in that way. Maybe Ronnie tried to rape her or something. David was the only person who could control her, and that was impossible now. Chris may have been able to mislead her by exploiting the relationship between him and David, but he was dead. The only other person that would be able to have any type of influence on her would be Tony, but making her bite a man's dick off was not Tony's style. In order for his plan to work, Detective Mathews had to find Felicia before the YBE, his crooked ass partner, or the rest of the police force did — and he intended to do just that.

Chapter 8

David sat in the lounge chair placed in the corner of Felicia and his hotel room the following morning. The newspaper he held in his hand began to crumple between his two fists. As the man read further, a grin formed on his face that almost reached from ear to ear.

"Well, baby, it looks like somebody took out old Mook for us. I'll bet a dollar to a bucket of shit that it was our good buddy Daniel. That only leaves three more people that have to be dealt with. Daniel, Tony, and that punk ass cousin of yours, Michael Mathews," David said in an extremely happy voice.

"Three more, my ass! This shit is over for me. I refuse to do it anymore. Besides, what makes you think that I would kill my own cousin?" Felicia yelled.

"Because I said you will. We've come this far, baby, now let's finish this thing and get on with our lives. I promise after this we can finally rest. You know I need you," David said, rubbing his fingertips up and down Felicia's arm.

"Not this time, you bastard!" Felicia yelled while pulling away from her husband. "You watched me put my mouth on another man's dick last night. You fuckin' made me bite that man's dick off! All for your sick little pleasure. This journey for revenge that I allowed you to drag me on ends right now."

"It ends when I say it ends," David yelled.

"Or what, motherfucker? You gonna kill me too? Go ahead, you son of a bitch; my soul is already dammed anyway because of you. I have nothing else to live for. My husband treats me like a cross between a trained pit bull and the average prostitute, I have committed horrible acts that I know the Lord will never forgive and even if He does, the memory of those things will haunt me forever and to top it all off, I don't know who saw me leave the bar with Little Ronnie. For all I know, I could have a fuckin' warrant out for my arrest."

"Baby, stop worrying. The police aren't looking for us. It would be all on the news if they were. We don't have anything to worry about," David said in an attempt to calm his wife.

"No, motherfucker, you don't have anything to worry about. It was me seen at the bar, not you. It is my fingerprints at DeJuan and Chris's house, not yours. As a matter of fact, you have managed to stay in the clear on this whole sick, twisted trip, and I allowed it. Well, no more. I refuse to be your sexy little hit woman any longer. As a matter of fact, I refuse to stay around you any longer," Felicia yelled as the thought of all the week's past events ran through her head all at once.

"You are gonna do what the fuck I tell you to and that's that," David demanded. "You seem to think that you have a choice in the matter. The only choice that you have is whatever choice that I make for you. Now I suggest you get that pretty little wig of yours on straight and remember who is running shit around here."

"Not this time, David. From this point on we are finished," Felicia said while putting on her jacket and heading toward the door.

"So you are just gonna leave me now, huh? What about what they did to me? I guess that doesn't matter anymore. You know I can't do this shit without you. I'm sorry for the way that I have been treating you. You know you mean the world to me. It's just that those fuckers that I thought were my friends and looked at like family literally destroyed my life. We have to make them pay, baby. What about all the plans we had together that can never take place now because of Daniel and his little peons? Just these last three, baby, and that's it. I promise," David begged his wife.

"But why Michael?" Felicia asked with tears falling down her face. "He's not even part of the YBE anymore. He hates them just as much as you do, and he is my cousin."

"Because I never could stand that punk ass motherfucker. The sooner that bastard is dead, the better. It makes no sense to go on a killing spree without killing the super cop of Columbus."

David's words burned right through Felicia's soul. She had almost fallen for the sad act that her husband was pulling on her, just as she had so many times before. The

YBE had screwed him over good and she knew that she was the only key to his revenge. She started to feel as if they deserved their fate for what they had done to her husband. Just as she was starting to become weak and give in to David, the thought of her cousin and what her husband wanted her to do to him crossed her mind. His beef with Michael was not even about revenge, only dislike. She had chosen David over her own flesh and blood once before, and refused to do it again.

"I'm sorry, but I can't do this anymore," Felicia said as she ran out of the hotel room.

David slowly bent over to tie his shoelaces, then went out the door after his wife. He was not worried about losing her, because he knew exactly where she was going. Felicia, on the other hand, was running as fast as she could. She knew that David was behind her even though she did not see him. After exiting the parking lot of the Knight's Inn and passing the Red Lobster located next door, she ran up Hamilton Road. David followed her at a slow pace. His patience was beginning to grow short with his wife. Her emotions were unnecessary to him. After all the crying and running, she would never be able to leave him, and the sooner she accepted that the better, in his opinion. This was a fact that Felicia was not willing to accept. She had every intention of eluding her husband today. She continued to run down Hamilton Road until she reached Eastland Mall. Before entering, she looked back to see her husband still on her trail with a cigarette hanging from his mouth. She ran inside the mall, past the food court to the bathroom located at the end of the hall. The ladies' room was kind of crowded, which made for a perfect hiding spot from her persistent husband. She kneeled down to look under the stall in an attempt to find an empty one. What she saw almost made her faint. The sight of her husband's Adidas in the stall directly in front of her. David pushed the door to the stall open with a grin.

"Can we end this now and go back to the room?" he asked in a sarcastic voice.

All of the woman in the restroom watched as the hysterical woman ran down the hall, through the food court, and further into the mall. Felicia was beginning to feel trapped. She had to get away from David. After continuously looking back and not spotting the man hunting her, she ran into the JC Penney department store located on the opposite end of the mall. She quickly grabbed a dress off of a hanger and entered the dressing room with the article of clothing. Felicia closed her eyes and leaned up against a wall.

"I really don't like that color. Why don't you try this one," David said while standing behind Felicia holding a different dress.

"Noooo!" Felicia screamed, falling to the floor. "Why are you doing this to me? Please leave me alone."

"I can't, baby. I need you. Things would be a lot easier if

you'd just accept the fact that I'll never leave you alone. You belong to me forever. Now let's get out of here before the police show up," David suggested in a calm voice.

"All right, I'll leave with you, but no more killing. I can't do it anymore. I know that I promised to be a loving and devoted wife, but I just can't do it anymore," she begged in a frantic voice.

"Sure you can, sweetheart. Just three more and it will all be over."

"No the fuck I can't, David!" Felicia yelled.

"If you loved me you would do it."

Those were the only words David had to say in order to convince his wife to carry out his plans. Since the day the couple met, Felicia could not resist the challenge of proving her love to David. As she exited the dressing room the entire department store was starring at her. The manager of JC Penney had alerted the police just seconds before her departure. Officer Brian Black was the first to respond to the call. Upon seeing Felicia, a giant smile appeared on his face. He followed her through the mall and into the parking lot. Although Brian's presence went undetected by Felicia, David was fully aware of the police officer following them.

"I think your little temper tantrum has gotten the attention of that crooked ass Officer Black," David said in an upset voice. "We have to make it back to the hotel."

"Oh my God!" Felicia responded. "Do you think he

∽ 40 ∽

knows what we've done?"

"He knows something, or else he would not be following us."

David and Felicia were not the only ones being followed. Detective Michael Mathews had been trailing his partner the entire morning. He knew that Brian would be on the hunt for Felicia. Just as Brian started to move in on Felicia, Detective Mathews intervened.

"Good morning, partner," Michael said as both officers pulled their cars in the path of Felicia. "Long time no see, cousin."

"What's the emergency?" Felicia asked in a frantic voice.

David had decided to test his wife's ability to handle this situation on her own. He ducked between two parked cars without being noticed by either officer. Brian was shocked to see his partner. The thought of Michael knowing about his misdeeds was the first thing to enter his head. His brain was racing to come up with an excuse as to why he was there and why he did not notify his partner about finding Felicia.

"A call came in over the radio about a hysterical woman inside of JC Penney — and look who I found in the parking lot. Mrs. Felicia Taylor!" Brian said in the most convincing voice he could come up with.

Felicia's heart felt like it was going to jump out of her chest. Her eyes were glued to her husband kneeling down between the two parked cars. His intentions were unknown to her. She refused to believe that he was going to just let her take the fall. *He has to have some kind of plan,* she thought to herself. Another thought that raced through her head was whether the plan her husband had included killing her cousin right now. Normally she would trust that her husband would not be foolish enough to attempt an attack on two police officers in the middle of Eastland Mall's parking lot at 3:30 in the afternoon, but nothing had been normal lately.

Brian was still puzzled about his partner showing up out of nowhere. He knew there was no way he would be able to deliver Felicia to Daniel with her cousin present. He had to get rid of the detective, but how? His thoughts were interrupted by the conversation between Felicia and Michael.

"Someone has been killing off all of your little buddies," Detective Mathews said.

"I heard," Felicia responded, trying to remain calm. "Little Ronnie and Mook were both in the paper this morning. I heard about DeJuan on the news yesterday."

"So I guess you don't know about Chris?"

"No! Is he all right?" Felicia asked in a surprised voice.

"If you consider dead all right. Listen, we need to talk. Either you can come by my place, or let me know where you are staying and I'll come by yours."

The situation was working out perfectly for David.

Felicia would be able to carry out his plans for the detective a lot easier than he'd thought. All she had to do was arrange the meeting and carry out the plan. The detective had plans of his own. By the worried look on his partner's face, he knew that Brian had no intention of letting Felicia show up at any type of meeting between the two.

"I was going to take her down to the station, sir," Officer Black said.

"No need for that. We can discuss this right here and now. I need you to find Tony and let him know that his boss Daniel just called me and said he witnessed him kill all three men murdered in the past few days. He also told me that Tony paid for the assassination of Little Ronnie," the detective said, pulling a cigarette from his pack.

David stayed in his hiding place wondering just what the detective had up his sleeve. Daniel knew nothing about the murders — and even if he did, why would he tell Michael Mathews? Brian was also wondering what was going on in his partner's head.

"We have not spoken in years. Why the hell would I be interested in delivering any type of message for you?" Felicia questioned.

"Because you are wanted for the murder of a police officer and I am the only one that can help you," Michael said with a sinister grin.

"What fucking police officer?" Felicia yelled, with a puzzled look on her face.

"This one!" the detective responded as he pulled a .38 snub nose from his waistband and fired a shot into Brian Black's forehead.

The shot echoed through the entire parking lot. Felicia could not believe her eyes. Her cousin had just killed his partner and planned to pin the murder on her. She could no longer wait around to see what David had planned. With all the speed her little body could produce, she ran out of the parking lot.

"Run, you little bastard, run!" the detective yelled while firing three more shots in the direction of Felicia, but purposely missing.

David stayed in his hiding spot long enough to hear the detective call in the murder and watch the Columbus Police Department respond. What shocked him the most was that he did not blame the shooting on Felicia as he had threatened. Instead he placed another pistol in Brian's hand and said he had to shoot his partner to keep him from assassinating a Ms. Felicia Taylor. Michael Mathews also had the recordings of his crooked partner's conversations with Daniel to back his story.

The police were so wrapped up in the shooting of one police officer by another fellow officer that they did not notice David strolling away from the scene of the crime. The events that had just taken place were very puzzling to him.

What the hell does that damned Michael have up his sleeve?

he thought to himself. *I may have to leave him alive long enough to find out. Besides, I'm starting to like his style.*

David did not go back to the Knight's Inn, because he knew that Felicia was not there. He lit a cigarette while walking up Hamilton Road toward Livingston. With the exception of his hysterical wife, all of his plans were coming together. Finding Felicia was not a concern, but finding Daniel was. David knew that the leader of the YBE would not be foolish enough to stay at his home with all of his crew dropping off like flies.

"I guess I'm just going to have to find a way to make Ol' Daniel come to us. Nine times out of ten he'll bring that punk ass Tony with him. Since the detective has such a hard-on for Tony, we can let him in on the meeting. This way we can kill three birds with one stone," David said with a grin.

David continued to walk, with a look of determination on his face, for the next two hours. He was convinced that he had thought of a way to make Daniel come to him. All he needed now was his wife to carry out his plan.

Chapter 9

Tony stepped out of the shower, grabbed the towel off the toilet, and proceeded to dry off. His better judgment told him to get away from everyone, so he checked into a room at the Fairfield Inn on Morse Road. He had spent the last two days there watching the news and trying to piece together not only the murders of his brother and friends, but all of the events that had taken place in the past few days. After seeing Michael gloating all over the news about shooting his crooked partner, he knew the streets were not the place for him at this time. Tony was a veteran of the streets and he not only knew how to play his cards, but when to play the game. He also knew that Daniel was just as skilled in the chess game of the streets as he. Together over the years they had managed to build an organization of ruthless, business-minded thugs which were unstoppable. Although Daniel was the self-proclaimed leader, Tony played a major role in founding and organizing the Young Black Entrepreneurs. He basically allowed Daniel to play leader because of some of the connections he possessed. As the years went by and Daniel realized the power that the title of leader carried, he invested more and more of his personal earnings into the organization, which pleased the connections and eventually cemented his position as leader. He showed no remorse about bumping Tony down from partner to employee. In fact, at times he even bragged about it, but never to Tony's face. Although described as an intelligent gentleman, Tony was just as quick-tempered as the rest of the lunatics that surrounded him. The thing that separated him from the rest was that Tony's fits of rage were done while he was completely sober, versus the drunken actions of basically all of his friends. That was the reason people tended to take him more seriously than the others. What made Daniel fear him the most was the fact that Tony was the only one that could control the crew. Although Daniel was the leader, he had about as much control over his crew as his grandmother would. For this reason, Daniel had to keep Tony happy. If not, the rest of the crew would be completely unmanageable. He even feared that if a member of the organization decided to assassinate him, no one would stop it from happening. In his opinion, keeping the identities of his connections a secret was what had kept him alive this long. Just as much as he needed the YBE, they needed him the same amount. That meant there must be coexistence between Daniel and Tony.

This had been Tony's train of thought for the past few years. He had grown content with letting Daniel play the big man. His job was easy and the pay was sufficient. But things were starting to change now. Tony's world was crumbling because of his brother's death. Although Chris and he were complete opposites, the two were extremely close. Chris was only one year younger than Tony, but was always treated like the little brother. Chris was bigger and a lot more athletic than Tony, but nowhere near as intelligent. The younger brother was more of the follower type that would easily get caught up in the moment and commit acts that he would later regret. He experimented with whichever designer drug was in style at the moment and often chose to make enemies rather then friends. Tony, on the other hand, believed that it was easier to catch flies with honey than with vinegar. Although being able to hold his liquor quite well had been a skill of his since the age of thirteen, Tony very seldom drank and never used a drug stronger then marijuana. Being a man of few words was the six-foot, light-skinned, clever man's style.

As Tony pulled a Newport out of the half empty pack of cigarettes lying on the night stand and lit it, his cell phone began to vibrate. The call was coming from a private number. He decided to let the phone ring and send the caller to the voice mail. Within seconds the cell phone vibrated shortly to alert him of a message just being recorded.

Who in the hell could that have been? He wondered as he entered his pass code into the phone in order to retrieve the message.

"Tony! It's me, Felicia! Please call me back at 777-9311. This is very important. Call back as soon as possible," the hysterical voice blared through the cell phone.

Tony dialed the number with one hand as he took one

last drag and then squashed the cigarette butt into the ash-tray with his free hand. A male voice answered the phone and notified him that he had dialed the Hamilton Road Knight's Inn, and asked him for the room number he was trying to reach. Tony hung up the phone with a puzzled look. As he wondered why Felicia did not leave a room number, his cell phone began to vibrate again.

"What up, doe?" Tony said as he heard Felicia's voice on the other end of the phone.

"I need to talk to you in person, Tony. It is very impor-tant. Can we please meet somewhere?"

"Where did you have in mind?" he asked as a wrinkle began to form on his forehead.

"I don't care. You pick the place. I just need to talk to you."

"How about Game Works out in Easton? I can be there in about an hour."

"You know I don't have a goddamn car. How in the hell do you expect me to get all the way out in Easton?" Felicia yelled.

"I can come pick you up. Where are you?"

"I don't think that would be a good idea," Felicia said as thoughts of her crazy cousin and deranged husband ran through her head.

"Well just what the fuck do you want me to do?" Tony said in a slightly aggravated voice.

"Just go there and I'll find a way," Felicia said with the

same aggravation in her voice.

"I'm there in an hour."

"OK, I'll be there. If you don't see me in an hour, then just wait for me. I promise I will be there."

"I got you, baby. See you in a minute."

"Tony!" Felicia yelled in an attempt to catch him before he hung up the phone.

"Yeah!"

"Make sure you bring your gun."

Tony hung up the phone without responding to her. Although he had just finished a cigarette, he could not resist the urge to smoke another one. His mind was going in a million directions at once after the phone conversation he just had. Felicia and he had been close since they were kids. There was even a time when he might have even been in love with her, but ignored his feelings out of respect for the friendship between him and David. Until today, Tony would have never thought there would come a time when his instincts told him not to trust Felicia. He had a very weird feeling about all of this, and with all of the events of the past few days, he knew he couldn't afford not to trust his instincts. After wrestling with himself for twenty minutes, Tony's curiosity got the better of his instincts. He placed his pistol on his side, left the hotel room, and got into his car.

Meanwhile, Felicia was racking her brain trying to figure out how she was going to get to Easton. Although she did not have much money to begin with, the little she had was now lost along with her purse, after being chased in the parking lot of a mall the previous day first by her husband, and then her cousin. She was also missing one shoe along with her purse. She had run several blocks before even noticing that her shoe was gone and the skin on the exposed foot was shredded. The unbearable pain in her foot, along with extreme exhaustion, made Felicia return to the Knight's Inn. Her prayers were answered when she awoke the next morning and realized that she was still alone in the hotel room. She cleaned her foot as best as she could and called Tony. Now she had to find a pair of shoes, make it to Easton, and make sure she was not being followed, all within an hour. Her life was turning into a giant nightmare. David was trying to make her kill half of the city and Michael wanted to frame her for the murder of a police officer. She sat on the edge of the chair, staring out the window, daydreaming of the day when all of this would be over. Felicia's thoughts were interrupted by the realization of how she could get to Easton. She saw an elderly couple in the parking lot loading bags into a red minivan from the room next door. She stood up on one leg, trying not to place any pressure on the injured foot. As the couple entered the room to retrieve more bags, Felicia ran to the van and dove into the driver's seat, completely ignoring her foot. Tears poured down her face as she jerked the van into reverse, backed out of the parking spot, then speeded out of the exit. Instinctively she had slammed her injured foot to the gas pedal. The pain was almost unbearable, but stopping was not an option. The speedometer of the minivan stayed between 78 and 80 miles per hour as Felicia weaved in and out of traffic.

I hope I can catch Tony in the parking lot, she thought as her right foot began to feel heavy and numb.

Her prayers were answered as she almost ran into Tony's car as they both tried to enter the lot at the same time. Tony parked his car as Felicia pulled right behind him.

"I need you to park this thing somewhere, run into the mall, and grab me a pair of shoes — then get me the hell outta here," Felicia said, limping to the passenger's side of Tony's car.

Tony did as requested without any hesitation or questions. He parked the van a few rows over and left the keys in the ignition. After a poor attempt to remove his fingerprints from the steering wheel with his shirt, he entered the mall, found a Foot Locker, and purchased a pair of Air Force Ones. While rushing back to the car, Tony received the shock of his life. He could not believe what he was seeing. David was dragging Felicia back to the stolen van that was parked a few rows over.

This is impossible! Tony said to himself.

Tony had been a logical man his whole life, but he could not come up with a logical answer for what his eyes were telling him. He was watching his dead best friend drag his wife through a parking lot. As much as he wanted to pursue the couple and get a closer look, his feet would not move from the spot where he was standing. The tires of the minivan squealed as David and Felicia sped away. This was one of the few times in Tony's life that he questioned his own sanity. The confused man slowly walked to his car and reached for the cigarette pack on the dashboard. He crumpled the empty pack in frustration. Another feeling began to come over him as he sat in the Easton parking lot trying to talk himself out of believing what he had just seen. He realized that Daniel was half right all along. Somebody was in fact declaring war on the YBE. Unfortunately where Daniel was wrong was that it wasn't Mook declaring war, it was David.

Chapter 10

A reflection of a fallen king is what the mirror gave as Daniel stared into it. The brown-skinned, medium-built man had been up for the past few days trying to figure out what his next move would be. Three of his most important foot soldiers had been murdered, and he hadn't heard from his bulldozer Tony since the night at Mook's. The police officer who had been on his payroll for years was also dead. For the first time in Daniel's life, he felt alone and helpless. With a drink in one hand and pistol in the other, he exited his bedroom headed for the kitchen. As he opened the refrigerator door looking for something to drink, his cell phone began to vibrate. A smile slid across his face as he recognized the number calling him.

"What up, doe?" Daniel answered in an eager tone.

"What's going down, big baby?" a deep voice with a slow midwestern drag groaned out of the cell phone that Daniel held to his ear.

The voice on the phone belonged to a local gangster who was known only by the name of Hustler. The name was a perfect fit for him because a hustler in every sense of the word was exactly what he was. He stood about six feet tall and weighed around 400 pounds. He was a very pleasant-spirited man who loved to eat. The success of his prostitution ring, loan sharking, after-hours spots, and small investments in a few mom and pop businesses — along with being responsible for a large part of the Franklin County drug problem — had enabled him to live rather comfortably. The act of the Hustler enjoying the fruits of his labor in public could not be mistaken for unawareness. The huge man could never be found without the two large 40 caliber Desert Eagle hand guns holstered on both his sides. The two pistols had never been fired to date. No one ever made it past the number of unknown bodyguards he hid around him at all times. Daniel had been doing business with the Hustler for the past ten years. There was no bad blood between them and he had no reason to feel threatened, but for some reason he did. It was more of an alone feeling that came over the leader of the most powerful group of gangsters in Columbus. There was no time for emotional sucka attacks now. This was the call he had been waiting for all month.

"Same shit, different day!" Daniel responded.

"That situation we discussed last month just took place. We need to get together and talk numbers. I'm at H. Johnson's on Whittier and Lockborne. Bring what you are in the negative on, and we can conversate about the new ticket."

The way that the Hustler talked to Daniel burned his soul. Although the two would often eat out of the same bowl, the Hustler would always make it known that he was the founder of the feast.

This fat motherfucker watches too many rap videos, Daniel thought to himself as he clenched the cell phone tighter. "I'll be there in about thirty minutes. Order me a monster pork chop sandwich with cheese."

"In a minute, big baby."

Although the Hustler was more financially stable than the entire YBE at the moment, he wanted no quarrel with them. His money was too long to stop flowing, and that was the only reason for his continuing existence. The YBE ran the streets and could easily eliminate the Hustler the moment he proved to be unprofitable. The idea of this was sounding better and better to Daniel after each one of their phone conversations. The only problem was that he didn't know how his crew was reacting to Tony leaving and not coming back for the past few days. Without Tony at his side the world, including his own crew, would take a piece of Daniel's ass. The proud leader decided to put his previous plans of getting rid of Tony to the side, for the time being. With Officer Brian Black dead now, it would be almost impossible for Daniel to continue to run the crew without Tony.

Hopefully Tony is somewhere laying low, and that damn Michael Matthews hasn't gotten a hold of him yet, Daniel thought to himself as he dialed Tony's cell phone number.

❖

The phone rang four times before going to the voice mail. Tony recognized the number was coming from Daniel's house and purposely ignored the call. His paranoid feelings about Daniel had taken a back seat to what he witnessed the day before.

I must be losing my fucking mind. David is dead. I saw him die, Tony thought to himself as a tear rolled down his cheek.

Tony lit fire to the half blunt that hung from his lips as he leaned back in the chair and stared at the wall. The smell of marijuana filled the room as Tony began to relive the night of David's death over in his head.

"I can't believe he's gone," Tony said in a low tone as he took another long drag of the marijuana.

Tony and David had been the tightest of the YBE crewmembers. The two had lived right next to each other since the day they both were born. Tony was the best man at Felicia and David's wedding and personally paid for their honeymoon to the Bahamas. The two were more than friends, they were like brothers. For that reason alone Tony always felt partly responsible for letting David die. Although he had nothing to do with his death, and would have prevented it if he had known what was going to take place, Tony placed the blame on himself. The only person more to blame than he was Daniel. Although Daniel had grown up with David, he always felt threatened by him and would much rather see him dead than alive. Tony was the smartest of the crew and probably could handle the position of leader better then anyone. David knew this and always tried to push Tony into taking the throne from Daniel. Tony

was satisfied with his position and often advised David to be satisfied as well. Instead of taking Tony's advice, David would verbally
express his disrespect for Daniel's authority to anyone who would
listen. Due to the fact that men gossip just like women, it didn't
take long for Daniel to get wind of David's feelings. He knew it
wouldn't be long before David got up enough nerve and stirred
up enough bullshit within the crew to start a mutiny. Daniel also
knew how close David and Tony were and that Tony would never go
for the assassination of David. So he cleverly planted seeds of David
being an informant for the police into the heads of DeJuan, Chris,
and a few other crew members. He explained to them that he tried
to convince Tony of David's betrayal, but couldn't make him believe
that his best friend was a snitch. The news was just as hard for the
other members of the YBE to believe. Daniel explained that he had
gotten this information from his cop on the take, Officer Brian
Black, and that David had been wearing a wire for the past two
years. He confirmed his story with a taped conversation between
David and Little Ronnie that took place inside Ronnie's truck. The
tape was actually recorded by Little Ronnie and given to Daniel
as proof of David's disrespect for the current leader and plans to
overthrow him. Daniel knew that DeJuan and Chris would be hard
to convince. He also knew that Chris always had a jealous-turned-
hate feeling for the relationship between David and his brother
Tony. Little Ronnie would ride with Daniel on this just because of
his ill feelings toward David. For DeJuan and the rest of the crew,
which wasn't very bright, the plan was perfect. The tape, recorded
by Little Ronnie but said to be a wire recording by David, was

all the convincing that the members of the YBE needed. At 4:30 a.m. on the morning of July 5th 2006, Chris, DeJuan, and Little Ronnie, along with ten other members of the YBE, led by their leader Daniel, arrived at the home of David and Felicia. Knowing that David was not going to go down peacefully, Daniel instructed his men to surround the house. DeJuan kicked in the front door while Little Ronnie kicked at the back. Five of the foot soldiers rushed inside the house with pistols in hand, followed by DeJuan and Daniel. Little Ronnie was still kicking at the reinforced back door. As DeJuan removed the thick piece of wood from across the back door and let Ronnie, Chris, and the other YBE members into the house, they heard two shots from upstairs. As three of the foot soldiers ran to the bottom of the stairs, they were faced with a furious David standing at the top of the staircase, holding a huge machine gun. He began to fire the automatic weapon while hollering cuss words at the intruders.

"Is that all you little bitches got? I hope you brought more then these two dead motherfuckers with you. I know you're down there, Daniel. Bring your punk ass up these stairs," David yelled while firing the machine gun.

As the shooting stopped, two of the foot soldiers rushed up the stairs, firing their weapons.

"Let's get this motherfucker," Chris whispered to Daniel, heading toward the stairs.

All of the lights were out and it was almost impossible to see where they were going. The eight remaining foot soldiers, plus Chris and DeJuan, were all upstairs now. Daniel and Ronnie remained at the bottom of the stairs until he was sure that David was captured.

"What the fuck are you doing?" Daniel asked with an aggravated tone. "Get your punk ass up there with the rest of them."

"Hell, it sounds like he's calling for you! Plus, you know that's not my thing," Little Ronnie responded. "I don't do all this Scarface type shit. Unless I get to wake his girl up and take her with me like Al Pacino did Michelle Pfeiffer."

"You ain't Pacino and she damn sure ain't Michelle Pfeiffer. Anyway, that bitch is gonna have to ride it out with her husband," Daniel said with an evil look on his face.

The ten members of the YBE carefully opened each door of the four-bedroom house in search of David and his wife. Two of the foot soldiers carefully entered the bedroom of David and Felicia as Chris followed closely behind. As soon as all three men were completely in the bedroom, David appeared from behind the door and shot one of the foot soldiers directly in the back of the head and the other in the arm. At the same time, a completely naked Felicia exited the closet with Rocky, the couple's huge pit bull. As the dog lunged at the throat of Chris, he fired two shots. Without regard for his fellow gang members, DeJuan fired three shots through the closed door. One of the bullets struck David in the middle of his back and the other two entered the back of the neck of the wounded foot soldier and out the front, leaving his head barely attached to his shoulders. David fell to the floor beside Chris and Rocky. The brave dog tried his best to protect his owners, but the shot that was delivered by Chris killed him instantly.

"Chris! What the fuck are you doing here?" Felicia yelled, surprised to see her and her husband's childhood friend.

"Pick up a gun and shoot that son of a bitch, baby," David moaned while trying desperately to drag the lifeless bottom half of his body toward the pistol that he had dropped.

David's words awakened Chris from the trance that Rocky's attack and the bullet- riddled bodies scattered around had placed him in. He pushed the corpse of the pit bull off of him and tried to beat Felicia to the pistol lying about six feet away from both of them. With incredible speed, Felicia leaped across the room onto the pistol before Chris could get to it. The carpet burned her knees as she tried to spin around and save her husband. She was met with the right hand of Chris crashing into her temple and knocking her unconscious. At the same time, DeJuan slammed his size twelve Timberland boot into the wounded back of David.

"Where the fuck do you think you're going?" DeJuan yelled in an aggravated tone.

"I swear, I'm gonna kill every last one of you bastards," David yelled as tears flowed down both sides of his face.

"Funky bitch!" Chris mumbled as he delivered a vicious

kick to the ribs of Felicia's lifeless, naked body.

"Please! Leave her alone, you motherfucker," David begged. "How could you do this? You grew up with the both of us. Both of you did. That punk ass Daniel is just using both of you. How long do you think it will be before either of you are in this very same position?" the bleeding man tried to reason.

"Sounds like the boys are playing a little rough with old David," Daniel looked over at Little Ronnie and said while heading up the stairs.

David somehow knew that this day would come sooner or later. He was never one to fear death, but this was not how he imagined it. His bedroom was filled with the re-maining six foot soldiers, Chris and DeJuan. His wife lay in the corner naked and unconscious while he lay para-lyzed and bleeding to death. He never cared for DeJuan too much, but tolerated him because of the years they had known each other. David did not like Chris at all, but the thought of harming or letting anyone else harm his best friend's little brother never entered his mind. He always knew about Chris's jealous feelings toward his and Tony's relationship but never thought it would come to this. In a weird sense, he did not even have any hard feelings toward DeJuan and Chris. They were Daniel's peons and never had a mind of their own, so he really didn't expect any different from them. There was something in his heart, though, that made him believe Tony would never betray Felicia and him this way. For that reason, he dialed Tony's number while he was hiding behind the door, and placed the cell phone in the waste basket.

"Your bitch ass boss doesn't have enough nuts to look me in my eyes before I die?" David asked, coughing up blood.

"Oh, I have intentions of doing more than looking you in the eyes before you die," Daniel said as he and Little Ronnie walked into the bedroom. "I plan on doing the honors of sending you on your sorry ass way."

As Daniel pulled his giant .45 Desert Eagle pistol from his full-length trench coat, he was interrupted by the sound of screeching tires in front of the house.

"It's Tony!" Ronnie said while looking out of the bedroom window.

"Good! He needs to see this," Daniel responded.

Tony jumped out of his car almost before it stopped moving. With cell phone still in hand, he ran inside the house and up the stairs. The sight of nine men standing around his best friend with guns pointed at him and Little Ronnie running his hands between Felicia's legs while she lay naked and unconscious sent a feeling of rage through his entire body. He lunged at Daniel, but was cut off by his younger brother Chris.

"This motherfucker is a snitch dog," Chris yelled, trying to justify their reasoning for this attack to his brother.

Tony pushed his brother off of him and hit Little Ronnie

who seemed to be in his own world with Felicia — in the face as hard as he could. Ronnie fell to the floor between Felicia and Rocky's corpse. He knew better than to try to fight Tony back or even get up for that matter. Tony would literally beat him to death and no one would be able to stop him.

"Get your fat, perverted ass off of her!" Tony yelled while turning back to confront Daniel and Chris. "What the fuck do you mean he is a snitch? David would rather die before he helps some punk ass police officer. This is all your doing, Daniel," he said while heading toward him again.

"Listen with your own ears," Daniel said while pushing play on the mini recorder and throwing it on the bed. "He tried to set Ronnie up a few weeks ago."

"Tony, you know me, dog," David said in a low tone. "It really doesn't matter. The damage is already done. This bastard knew he was gonna have to get rid of me and I guess he didn't have enough nuts to face me himself, so he had to come up with some bullshit story about me, of all people, being a snitch. Just be careful around this snake ass nigga, Tony, and don't let them hurt Felicia anymore," David begged, coughing up more blood.

"If any one of you bitches touches him or her again, I'll kill you," Tony yelled in anger. "If you plan on killing him, Daniel, then you're gonna have to kill me first."

"Too late!" Daniel said as he fired a shot right into the back of David's head.

"Nooooo!" Tony screamed as he fell to the floor.

All of the men walked out of the bedroom and down the stairs, except for Chris who took a knee beside Tony and David's corpse.

"It had to be done, bra. You heard the fucking tape. What else were we supposed to do?" Chris asked his big brother, desperately wanting his approval.

"Get the fuck away from me!" Tony growled.

Chris stood up and headed toward the door. Before exiting he took one look back at the carnage that he helped cause. He couldn't help but feel a little remorse for what had took place tonight. Despite of his jealous feelings for David, the man had always treated him like a brother. Deep down inside, he knew David was not a snitch and even if he was, Felicia didn't deserve this. It would take a lot of Hennessy and weed to make him forget about this night.

Tony wrapped Felicia up in a sheet and carried her to his car. After placing her inside, he opened the trunk and got the exact same can of gas from the episode at Mook's, entered the house and headed back upstairs. His mind was blank at this point. If David was working for the police, then Daniel's actions were justified. If not, then he'd just watched the assassination of his best friend and couldn't do anything about it. He suddenly faced the reality that he was never going to know the truth. As Tony splashed the gasoline all over the bedroom, David's last words began to tattoo themselves into his mind. David seemed to be more concerned with Tony watching his ass around Daniel and the safety of Felicia than he was with saving his own life. It was for that reason that Tony has never trusted Daniel again. He lit the match, threw it into the house, and watched the flames as memories of his best friend ran through his mind. As he climbed into his car, Tony looked over at Felicia. He drove over to Grant Hospital and laid Felicia on the ground outside of the emergency room.

The blunt Tony was smoking burned out in the ashtray. With a frown on his face, he got out of the chair and dialed Daniel's number. He had made up his mind that David was haunting him for letting him die. There was only one way for his best friend to rest in peace and for him to go on with his life, and that was to kill Daniel.

Chapter 11

Smoke filled the air as Felicia lit her cigarette with a cigarette she already had burning. She stared at her husband, lying asleep on the bed, and contemplated different ways to kill him. The man of her dreams had become the star of her nightmares. The woman tried to stand, but instantly fell upon placing pressure on the shredded right foot, which was now swollen to twice its normal size. She screamed in pain while lying on the floor. With suicidal thoughts running through her mind and tears forming a small puddle on each side of her head, Felicia allowed her head to fall and dazed under the bed. She noticed a book lying next to her, slightly under the bed, and picked it up. It was a book of poetry written by a lady named Tameka Bowman. She opened the first page and saw a picture of the young author. The girl appeared to be a teenager. Felicia's thoughts were confirmed when she read the "About the author" section and found out that she was a fifteen-year-old high school student, right here in Columbus, Ohio. She opened the book dead in the center and began to read the poem.

"Lost"

Have you ever felt like you were lost?
Like you were all alone?
Like you have nobody there for you?
Even when you have family and friends or a loved one in your life?
With friends, family, and your lover are you still lost?
Well, I do!
Have you ever felt like you were lost?
Like the world is too big for you?
Like one day you will scream out, "I want my mom, I want to go home, I don't want to be lost."
Well, I do!
Have you ever felt like you were lost?
Like everything in your life was so good then you find out it was a dream.
Like it was all in your head?
Like you were so fucking lost you don't know what to do?
Well, I do!
So tell me — have you ever felt like you were lost?

The poem seemed to touch something inside of Felicia. Despite all the problems she had going on in her life, she wondered what could have made this fifteen-year-old girl feel this way. She felt a certain desire to find the author and talk to her. Maybe give her a hug and tell her that everything would be all right once she became an adult. It was at that moment that Felicia's own problems entered her head. How could she possibly entertain the thought of telling some troubled teen that everything is going to be all right when she knew for a fact that it wasn't? Life was fucked up and it didn't seem to be getting any better. In fact, it seemed to be getting worse by the minute.

"Hell, I need to find this little chick and see if I can inspire her next poem," Felicia mumbled to herself as she made another attempt to stand.

Pain shot through her foot like lightning bolts. The current state of the young woman's life was really wearing on her sanity. Felicia yelled David's name as loudly as she could.

"What!" David yelled back in an aggravated tone.

"I've got to pee."

"What are you telling me for?" "Because you've got to move that fat bastard out of the bathroom," Felicia responded in a tone that was just as frustrated as David's.

David jumped out of the bed and stomped to the bathroom. He looked down at the bloody beaten body of the Hustler and thought of how clever his plan was. All he had to do was sit back and wait for Daniel to show up for the meeting between him and the Hustler, and then receive his gift of revenge. Kidnapping the large kingpin was easier than he thought. His bodyguards were not as tough as they portrayed themselves to be, either. One look at David made all of them piss their pants. Knowing that moving the large man would be almost impossible for Felicia, David decided to make the Hustler as comfortable as possible by holding him hostage in his own house. After all, Felicia was in need of a shower and he could use a nap and was sure the Hustler had a nice comfortable bed. Besides, Daniel would feel a lot more comfortable meeting at the Hustler's home front. Getting the kingpin to make the phone call to Daniel was even easier. It's amazing what people will agree to when threatened by a person whose funeral they have already attended.

"This is all you had to do," David yelled as he slid the shower curtain closed.

"He'll hear me!" Felicia yelled with extreme anger in her voice.

"The sound of you pissing is the last thing on this fat motherfucker's mind!" David yelled in the same tone.

"I fuckin' hate you!" the angry woman yelled as she slammed her body down on the toilet.

Detective Michael Mathews sat in his car three houses down from Daniel's home. He figured either Tony would be showing up there soon in a fit of rage after hearing the message Felicia delivered to him, or Daniel would be heading out to find Tony and come up with a plan. Either way, the whole YBE empire had been turned upside down and the detective knew staking out Daniel's house would be his best move. The street was pretty quiet for a Thursday night, and all the lights were off inside the house. He had been posted there for the past four hours and his thighs were beginning to burn from sitting down for such a long time. Just as soon as the detective opened his car door so he could stretch his legs, he spotted Daniel heading toward his car alone with a large duffel bag in his hand. The chubby detective quickly ducked back down into the car and watched as the green Cadillac sedan that Daniel drove headed down the street.

"Finally! I knew something was going to shake around here sooner or later. Let's see where the fearless little leader is gonna take us tonight," Michael said as he lit a cigarette and slowly began to follow Daniel.

The detective followed Daniel to the Fairfield Inn located on Morse Road. It wasn't long before Michael spotted Tony coming out of the hotel, headed for Daniel's car. He leaned in the window and held about a two-minute conversation before getting into the car. Once again the detective followed as the car drove off. He had to resist the urge to ride up on the side of the car and kill the both of them. Instead he had a better plan. He would follow them to their destination; kill the both of them and any other YBE member present, then get away clean with any money or drugs that might be involved. His only concern was whether Felicia had delivered the message to Tony. If not, the detective might have some issues carrying out his plan. Tony was always on his toes. There would be no way he could execute a sneak attack unless Tony was distracted.

Meanwhile, the car that the two YBE members rode in was full of tension. Even though Felicia never got to tell Tony about her cousin the detective, he still had his own reasons for not trusting Daniel. His senses were sharper than usual this night. He could not tell from the phone call that he received from Daniel earlier if this whole trip was a setup, or if the mighty leader really needed him. Those issues were the least of his worries. Tony had convinced himself that David was going to haunt him until he avenged his death. The only way to do that would be to kill Daniel. This task would be pretty simple for Tony physically. Even with ten years of training, Daniel would still not be able to outfight or outgun Tony, and both of them knew it. But what if he was wrong? What if after Daniel was dead David's soul still would not be at peace? What exactly did David have planned for him?

Maybe I'm just trippin', Tony thought to himself as he looked over at Daniel.

The thoughts that were running through Daniel's mind were even worse. He did not know what page his right-hand man was on. With all of the main members of his crew turning up dead, he didn't know who to trust right now. Was this all the Hustler's doing, and was this meeting between them going to be a trap? The fact of the Hustler calling and changing the location of the meeting to his house had Daniel's mind racing. The Hustler has always known he could not win a head up war with the YBE, but by killing all the key members one by one his position would strengthen. The thought of all this made Daniel think about his recently exterminated enemy, Mook. Did Mook use his last breath to tell the truth when he screamed his innocence? And what about Tony? Could he finally be plotting a takeover of the YBE? Did he go into a rage and start killing his own crew members after the death of Chris? Did Tony get wind of the plot he and the late officer Brian Black had planned for him? There was only one thing that Daniel was certain of, and that was the fact that tonight was going to be an extremely long and stressful night.

"Listen, I'm gonna need you to be on your Ps and Qs tonight. That fat bastard sounded kind of strange on the phone," Daniel looked over at Tony and said in an attempt to break the silence.

"You just handle your end and I'll take care of mine as usual," Tony responded without even looking over at Daniel.

"What's the deal with you lately? We got the motherfucker that killed Chris."

"Mook didn't kill Chris and you know it as well as I do," he snapped in an aggravated tone. "Once again I allowed you to use me for your own little personal vendettas."

"Well, I think we got the right man. And even if we didn't, Mook was going to have to go sooner or later anyway."

"So what am I supposed to do about the real murderer

of my brother?"

"If it wasn't Mook then I guarantee you that we will find the motherfucker that killed Chris and all the rest. We just have to be careful and lay low for a while, especially you."

"What the hell do you mean, especially me?" Tony asked with a wrinkle in his forehead.

"Not long before Detective Black was killed, he called me and said that Detective Mathews was expecting you to go on a killing spree over Chris. He figures you would clean up the streets for him by exterminating anybody of importance; then he could just arrest you," Daniel responded.

"Are you sure that was Detective Mathew's plan and not yours?" Tony said, without trying to hide the distrust in his voice.

"Get the fuck outta here! You know you're my main man. Take away all the money, cars, and jewelry and we still got a friendship that goes back to elementary school," Daniel said in a half-hurt tone, even though Tony's accusation was partly true.

"So did you and David!"

"That motherfucker was never my friend. You may have loved that snitch ass nigga but I didn't. Fuck him and the horse that he rode to hell on. If I had the chance I would kill his punk ass again!" Daniel screamed in extreme anger.

"Be careful what you wish for. You just might get the chance," he responded with a smirk on his face.

"And just what the fuck is that supposed to mean?"

"Nothing! I'm just trippin. Let's just get through this little meeting with the Hustler without any problems. Make sure you keep an eye on that fat motherfucker. I'll cover the outside," Tony said, pulling a Newport from his cigarette pack.

"Looks like it's just me and you again — just like the old days, huh? Stop worrying. We're gonna go in here and handle this shit and be out without any problems. You watch my back and I got yours," Daniel said as he stuck his fist over at Tony in an attempt to call a truce to their recent arguing.

Tony took his fist and hit the top of Daniel's, confirming that the two would work together, at least for tonight. He was at a crossroads in his life. Although he did not trust Daniel and was coming close to hating him, the two did have an extremely long relationship. With everyone else dead, each other was all that the two had left. He hoped that his encounter with David and Felicia was all a bad dream and that his dead best friend would remain dead. The thoughts he was having made him again question his own sanity. The only thing he was sure of was that tonight would defiantly be the deciding factor of his future. Although the two rarely saw eye to eye, Daniel had come to the same conclusion.

Chapter 12

A brown-skinned, heavyset lady by the name of Racquel sat at the end of her bed holding her daughter's picture. Her motherly instinct told her that Felicia was in trouble. Her daughter never recovered from the death of her husband and Racquel was extremely worried about her. She had not heard from Felicia in about a month, which was very unusual considering the two were very close. Seeing all of her daughter's friends on the news as murder victims only made her worries worse. She was determined another day would not go by without finding her daughter.

"Wake up! Wake up, Bubba!" Racquel insisted as she shook her boyfriend, who was lying next to her.

"What, baby?" he responded in a half-asleep tone.

"Come on. We're going to find Felicia. I've got the strangest feeling that my baby is in some kind of trouble."

"I guess you couldn't have gotten this feeling before I took a shower and got into bed for the night?" Bubba responded sarcastically.

"I swear, if you don't get your bald-headed, toothless ass out of this bed and take me to find my daughter, you will never get another peaceful night for as long as you live," the large woman threatened while standing over Bubba with her hands on her hips.

"I don't know why I put up with this shit!" Bubba mumbled under his breath as he stood up and began to put his clothes on.

Racquel and Bubba left the house headed for the home of Davonna McGill, the fiancée of DeJuan and best friend of Felicia. Racquel had known the woman since she was a child, and formed a close mother-like relationship with her. She knew that the young lady was going through a lot of pain over the death of her high school sweetheart, and felt kinda bad about this being the first visit she had paid her since the murder. Her sympathetic feelings did not distract her from the original mission she was on. If anyone knew where Felicia was, it would be Davonna. Bubba made a comment as to how deserted the house looked as Racquel pulled into the driveway. The two exited their vehicle and walked up to the door. As Bubba reached out to knock on the door it flew open forcefully.

"What the fuck are you doing here?" Davonna's mother Lisa yelled in an angry tone.

Racquel's mouth dropped. She was shocked at the words and the tone of them coming out of Lisa's mouth. The two parents had become quite close over the years.

"Why the hostility?" she responded with a puzzled look on her face as she looked over at Bubba and saw the same look of surprise.

"You've got some nerve showing up here after what your daughter did to Davonna."

"Lisa, please! I don't know anything that may be going on. I have not seen or heard from Felicia in a month. Everyone is turning up dead and I am extremely worried about her. I came here to see if Davonna may have talked to her. I need to know if my baby is all right!" Racquel pleaded, with tears streaming down her face.

Lisa could tell that the pain Racquel was feeling was not an act. The hurt of not knowing the whereabouts or well-being of a child that grew inside you for nine months is a pain that every mother feels when witnessing another mother go through it. Besides, she had been unable to get the straight of what happened between the two friends herself. The only thing she knew was that Felicia was somehow involved in the pain her daughter was feeling. Reluctantly, Lisa decided to calm down and invited Racquel and Bubba to come inside.

"I apologize, baby. I had no idea that you had not heard from your daughter. I really don't know what is going on. I have been over here since the night DeJuan was killed. Davonna has been a wreck ever since," Lisa explained with the same look of motherly concern as Racquel.

"I know Davonna has to be taking this pretty hard. Felicia has not been the same since David's murder. What did we let our babies get involved with?" Racquel cried as she sat on the couch with her head in her hands.

"You don't understand, Racquel. This is more then just taking it hard. Davonna has had a complete breakdown. She has not spoken a word since the night she burst into the house screaming."

"What are you talking about?" Bubba asked with a confused look on his face.

Lisa looked at the bald-headed man with disgust and rolled her eyes at him.

"I'm assuming Davonna saw DeJuan's murder. I never told the police or anyone else. I knew nobody could get to DeJuan unless that fuckin' Daniel ordered it, and I couldn't take any chances of my baby getting hurt. Hell, your daughter is damn lucky to be here."

"Oh my God. I had no idea Davonna saw it. What did she say happened?" Racquel asked with tears still rolling down her face as she remembered the night her daughter witnessed the same event.

"She has not said shit since that night. I guess she had some type of suspicion that DeJuan was cheating on her. She was hell bent on going over there to find out what was going on. I sat here for two hours trying to talk her out of going to that boy's house, but you know how crazy that damn Davonna is. About thirty minutes after she left, the door comes flying open and she's falling through it, muddy as hell. I jumped up so fast that I broke my damn toe on the corner of this heavy ass end table. Now the both of us were on the floor screaming. By the time I got over the pains shooting through my foot and got her to stop screaming and crying, the only thing that I could make sense out of was that DeJuan was dead and Felicia played some part. What part, I don't know."

"Get the fuck outta here!" Bubba said while standing in anger.

"No you can get the fuck outta my goddamn house, motherfucker!" Lisa yelled right back. "Racquel, I am very sorry about what you are going through, but my baby has not said a word since. I don't know what Felicia's involvement in all this is, but Davonna was scared to death that Felicia was going to come here and kill her. Now as a mother and a friend, I hope you didn't come over here for no bullshit?" Lisa screamed as she pulled a little snub nose .38 caliber pistol from her pocket and held it to her side.

"I don't give a shit about your little pea shooter!" Racquel responded in an angry tone. "Now as I expressed earlier, I am deeply sorry about Davonna's loss, but my own daughter experienced the same shit and I ain't accusing people or pointing any fingers, and I'm not about to let you stand here and slander my daughter's name."

"My daughter don't have not one motherfuckin' reason to bust in here, fall on the floor, and pretend to be scared shitless just to slander your daughter's name. Now this thing seems to be getting pretty ugly and I ain't gonna keep letting your punk ass man swell all up at me in my own house, so I suggest you two be going on your way," Lisa said, slightly raising the pistol in her hand.

"Go wait for me in the car, baby," Racquel looked over

at Bubba and said.

"Hell no! I'm not leaving you in here with this crazy bitch," he responded.

"Baby, please. I need to talk to Lisa. Go wait in the car. I'll be all right."

Racquel watched her man walk down the walkway, trying her best to control her emotions. She had to find out what was going on with her daughter. Although Lisa had made this a very unpleasant visit to say the least, she felt sorry for the frantic woman standing across the room from her with a pistol in her hand. She walked over to Lisa and hugged her. Instead of resisting, Lisa instantly hugged her back and the two women stood in the middle of the living room crying and holding each other.

Racquel, the first to break the silence, looked Lisa in the eyes and said, "I really need to talk to Davonna. I have to find out what is going on with my daughter. Please allow me to talk with her, Lisa."

"Like I said earlier, she has not said a word since that night, but you are more than welcome to try. Come on, I'll take you to her room," Lisa said while walking down the hall and placing her pistol back into her pocket. "Baby, Racquel is here to see you."

"Noooo!" Davonna screamed. "They're gonna kill me!" the hysterical woman insisted while jumping out of the bed and balling up into a corner.

"You see? This is the shit that I'm talking about. What

the fuck is going on with my daughter?" Lisa looked at Racquel and yelled.

"I swear to you, I don't know. Davonna baby, it's me, your Aunt Racquel. Please talk to me. Your mother is right here. It's just us three, baby," Racquel pleaded to the terrified girl.

"It's all right, baby. Mama is right here with you, sweetheart and I got my hand on the trigger in case we have some problems," Lisa assured her daughter with the confidence of a lion in the jungle.

Racquel was starting to get aggravated by all the indirect threats Lisa kept sending at her. After this thing was all over, Racquel had no plans of continuing her friendship with her. In fact, the thought of whipping her fat ass was beginning to sound better and better as the night went on. Her thoughts were interrupted by the sight of Davonna slowly unballing herself and crawling toward her. The motherly instincts of the worried woman made her fall to her knees and stretch her arms out at the sobbing young lady. Davonna leaped into Racquel's arms and released a cry that could be heard through the whole house.

"I know, baby," Racquel comforted. "Tell me what happened."

"DeJuan, they killed him. I saw them. I was looking into the window and I saw, I saw her killing him," Davonna cried as her whole body trembled from remembering the events of that night.

"Who baby? Who did you see?" Racquel insisted.

"Yeah, who was it, baby?" Lisa encouraged.

"It was Felicia and David!" Davonna cried. "I know David is dead, but I swear he was there with Felicia. I didn't see him but he was there, making Felicia help him kill my baby."

"What do you mean, you know he was there?" Lisa yelled angrily. "You went to David's funeral. You know he is dead. Maybe you saw someone else? It had to be someone else, baby, because David is dead."

"I fucking know he is dead, Ma! I didn't see him — but I did, at the same time. I mean there is no way that Felicia could have lifted, tossed, and thrown DeJuan around the room like that by herself. I watched my baby fly through the room like a rag doll. The whole time Felicia was begging and pleading for David to stop, but I never saw him. Then all of a sudden everything stopped and I watched her hug the air. She really was hugging the air, but in her mind it was David. She told him that she would always love him and do whatever he needed. Then she dove on my baby and kept cutting him. I could see DeJuan's face being hit without anyone hitting it. Then David or something threw him across the room. Soon as he landed, Felicia attacked him again. Racquel, you've got to fuckin' believe me," Davonna begged, looking Racquel directly in the eyes. "Felicia killed DeJuan, and David made her do it. David helped her, I swear."

Racquel wanted to become angry but she couldn't. She wanted to call Davonna every lying little bitch in the book and push her crazy ass off of her, but she couldn't. She wanted to get up and kick the shit outta both of these crazy bitches, pistol or no pistol, but she couldn't. She wanted to believe her daughter was innocent of everything she was accused of tonight, but deep down in her heart — for some reason, she couldn't. For some reason she believed every word that Davonna said.

Lisa, on the other hand, did not know what to believe. She had her daughter's back one hundred percent until David came into the story. Lisa was a very logical woman who lived strictly by facts and never opinions, and it seemed the facts were that her daughter had lost her mind. She claimed that her best friend, with her dead husband's ghost, killed DeJuan. A feeling of embarrassment began to come over her.

"I'm very sorry for all of today's events," Lisa said while wiping the tears away from her eyes. "My daughter seems to be a little delusional."

"No, everything is fine," Racquel replied while hugging and rocking Davonna like a huge child. "You wouldn't know where I could find Felicia at, would you, baby?" Racquel looked down at Davonna and asked in a low tone.

"Hell, no! I don't ever want to see her again. She killed my baby! She killed DeJuan!" Davonna sobbed.

As Racquel released Davonna and tried to stand, Lisa

extended her hand in an attempt to help the large woman to her feet and apologize at the same time.

"Is there anything I can do to help?" Lisa asked.

"No. I think you have been through enough. I'm going to call my nephew Michael and see if he can help me. I know he and Felicia have not been that close since she married David, but I'm still his favorite aunt. He'll help me find her," Racquel said with her head pointed at the ground. "Listen, I don't know what the hell is going on, but if my daughter is involved in this shit I want to —"

"Stop!" Lisa interrupted. "Don't say another word. I know how you must be feeling, and I want you to know that I'm here for you. Go find your daughter — and if you need me, just call," Lisa said, hugging Racquel as tight as she could.

Racquel exited the house and got into the car with her waiting boyfriend Bubba. There were a million thoughts going through her head all at once. She did not want to believe her daughter was a killer, but she knew Davonna was not faking. In that young woman's heart, Felicia had killed DeJuan. But Davonna also believed that David was there too and that was impossible. The only thing that Racquel knew for sure was that her baby was somewhere out there by herself and needed her help.

Chapter 13

The sun was beginning to set as the theme music to WWE's Monday Night Raw blared loudly from the television set. David sat in the huge specially made leather recliner, drinking a Corona while staring at his wife lying on the couch across the room.

"Baby, I know the past few days have been rough for you. Hell — the past few months, for that matter, but I swear this whole thing will be over after tonight."

"You said that right before DeJuan, Chris, and Little Ronnie," Felicia responded in a distrustful tone. "You seem to be enjoying all of this shit."

"You're goddamn right I'm enjoying this shit. These motherfuckers deserve their punishment twice! You were there! They came in our home and violated my wife, my manhood, and my entire existence. How the fuck do you expect me to respond?" David yelled in a tone that shook the whole house along with the Hustler and Felicia's soul.

Although extremely frightened, Felicia was hurting for her husband. Not because of what happened the night of his death, but for allowing his soul to be used as a tool for the devil. She was beginning to understand now that this was no longer her husband in front of her, but some kind of demon from hell.

"The man in the bathtub had nothing at all to do with what happened to us, David!" Felicia yelled at the top of her lungs. "He is innocent just like me."

"What the fuck do you mean innocent like you?"

"That's right, David. I didn't have anything to do with what happened that night, but you are punishing me right along with your enemies. I'm a double victim here. I was beaten within an inch of my life and when I awoke, I found out that the love of my life was dead!" Felicia cried as the tears dripped off of her chin and soaked into the bandages on her injured foot. "I prayed and prayed for the Lord to bring you back to me, but not like this. You are not the man I married."

"You know being betrayed, killed, having an autopsy performed on you, embalmed, stuffed in a casket, buried, and sent to hell tends to ware a man down," David responded in a sarcastic tone. "So please forgive me if my heart doesn't bleed for you. Besides, I thought it was me and you forever. I guess that was all just bullshit to you, huh? I came all the way back from the grave for you."

"You came back for your revenge, and that's it!"

"I deserve it!"

"Even at my expense?" Felicia yelled.

Despite what Felicia thought David, was at odds about all of the actions he had forced his wife to take. He was driven by something he could not explain. His whole new existence was a mystery to him. He had no answers for the present and the future seemed to be even cloudier. He loved Felicia and the sight of her in so much mental and physical pain hurt him. Or did it? Was this just some type of reminder of how he was supposed to feel when he was alive? Was he capable of hurting, loving, or any other type of emotion? Was he nothing more than just a demon from hell? Although he was under the impression that he still loved his wife, there was no way that she would get out of helping him carry out his plan. If that made him a demon, then so be it.

"Go make sure the porch light is on," David demanded. "I want it to look real peaceful when Daniel pulls up. I get the feeling he'll be bringing that dick-ridin' ass Tony with him. And your nosey ass, crocked, maniac cop of a cousin is probably following the two jackasses. That means we can get everybody all at once and this thing will be all over. We can get back to our normal life," David told his wife, knowing that nothing about him was or ever would be normal again.

"Sure, baby. Whatever you say," Felicia responded in a low voice as she limped into the living room and flicked on the light switch.

Felicia knew that there was no chance of escaping David. She wanted to cry again, but her eyes could not produce any more tears. Her husband had kidnapped her soul and had literally planned to drag her to hell with him. How did the Lord let this happen to her? What exactly was she being punished for? As these thoughts ran through her head and she began to wander through the Hustler's house, she noticed a small flashing light coming from a corner in the hallway. The light was from the Hustler's cell phone, which had been dropped during his abduction. Felicia quickly picked up the phone and began to dial her mother's number. The phone rang six times before an answering service picked up.

"Pick up the damn phone, Ma," Felicia cursed as she redialed the number.

The half-hysterical woman's palms were sweaty and her heart was beating out of control. A sense of hope entered into her mind. Felicia believed that finding the cell phone was the Lord's way of letting her know that He had not abandoned her. A piece of that hope left after every unanswered ring of her mother's phone.

"Is that my phone ringing?" Racquel yelled out to Bubba from the bathroom of their apartment.

"Yeah," Bubba responded while picking the cell phone up and handing it to Racquel through the half-closed bathroom door.

"Thank you, baby," the woman responded while searching for the talk button. "Hello?"

"Ma! It's me, Ma," Felicia whispered.

"Baby! I've been worried sick about you. Thank God you are alive. Where are you?" Racquel asked in an eager tone, running out of the bathroom.

"Mom, I need you Mom," she cried. "David has me and he won't let me go. I know this sounds crazy, Mom, but you got to believe me. He's making me do horrible things."

"I believe you, baby. Now tell me where you are, so I can come get you."

"Do you remember Old Man Fletcher's little brother Shawn? The big one that everyone calls the Hustler?" Felicia asked, turning around to make sure that her husband was not behind her.

"I think I know who you are talking about."

"Well, that's where —"

"Tell Mommy I said hello," David said, snatching the cell phone from Felicia and hanging it up.

"Baby! Baby!" Racquel yelled into the phone, knowing that the call had ended.

Before David could respond to his wife's betrayal, the cell phone began to vibrate. He looked at the screen and saw the call was coming from Daniel.

"What's going down, big baby?" David answered in the exact same voice as the Hustler.

"I'm coming down your street now. I'll be there in about two minutes."

"I hear you, big baby. The door will be open."

"Yep."

"Its show time, baby," David looked at Felicia and said. "Get your head together, because this is the big one. After this, baby, it will be all over. Now I know that all of this has been very stressful for you, but I swear on our marriage that after tonight everything will be back to normal. I need you, baby."

"You are dead, David!" Felicia yelled to her husband. "We can never be normal again."

"Dead or not, baby, I still love you," David responded in the most sincere tone he could. "Now the question is — do you still love me?"

"Of course I do."

"Then prove it!" David demanded as he walked into the bathroom and slid the shower curtain back.

Felicia looked down at the floor and asked the Lord for forgiveness under her breath. She knew that she had to finish the job. If David was determined enough to come back from the grave just to seek revenge, there was no way he would ever let her rest unless she helped him. The thin brown-skinned lady stood up as straight as she possibly could, ignoring the excruciating pain running through her foot. She walked into the bathroom without limping, pulled out the pistol that was used in the other murders, and checked the clip for a bullet count. After seeing that the clip was full, she shoved it into the pistol hard while looking at her husband. Felicia leaned over and kissed David passionately, with the Hustler looking up at the couple in fear.

"I love you, baby," Felicia said.

"I love you too. Now let's sit this fat motherfucker up to the table and go open the door. Our house guests are about to arrive," David said as he smacked his wife on the ass and gave her a look of approval.

Chapter 14

A feeling of déjà vu came over Bubba as he pulled into the driveway of Lisa and Davonna's home. He had an extremely bad feeling about the mission that he and Racquel were about to go on, but had no choice but to follow his woman's lead. For the second time in one night he watched Racquel get out of the car and walk up this raggedy driveway. Racquel was thinking the exact same thing as she knocked on the front door.

"Not to sound rude, but I think me and my family have seen as much of you as we can stand for one night!" Lisa said as she swung the door open with an exhausted look on her face.

"I know, baby, but please, you've got to hear me out. Can I come in, please?" Racquel begged.

The emotions of Lisa were running wild inside of her body. She was half concerned about Racquel and her situation but still cautious of the frantic woman. She realized that Racquel was a concerned mother but at the same time, she and her daughter might have been the cause of Davonna having a nervous breakdown and starting to see ghosts. Reluctantly Lisa stepped to the side and allowed Racquel to come inside.

"Thank you so much, Lisa. I'll always love you for supporting me now," the large woman said as tears ran down her cheeks.

"Well, I can support you better from a distance. So please get to the point so we can put some distance between us — at least for the next twenty-four hours, please!"

"I understand," Racquel said with her head down. "I only came back because I need you. My baby just called me! She was whispering! She says that David has her and was making her do awful things. Just like Davonna tried to tell us. While I was talking to her the phone just hung up. I swear, Lisa, I heard David's voice in the background."

"Now do you believe me?" Davonna yelled from the hallway.

"Go back to your room, baby," Lisa yelled.

"No, Mom! I told you that Felicia and David killed DeJuan! I told you that I was not crazy! You didn't want to believe me!" she yelled at the top of her lungs.

"You love upsetting my home, don't you?" Lisa looked at Racquel and said.

"Trust me, Lisa, that is not my intention."

"Well, why the hell did you come back here with this damn ghost story?"

"Because I need your help. Don't you have a cousin named Fletcher?"

"Yeah, I do," Lisa answered with a confused look on her face.

"Does he have a younger brother named Shawn?"

"What does the Hustler have to do with this?" Davonna yelled out again from the same spot.

"That's the name she used! The Hustler!" Racquel yelled in an excited tone. "My baby said that's where they were at."

"I still need to know — what the fuck do you expect from me or my daughter?" Lisa responded in an angry tone. "I know I said I would be here for you if you needed anything, but usually people don't accept those types of offers. Especially within the next couple of hours."

"Would you please direct me and Bubba to your cousin's house? That's it. I just need to get my daughter. Please!" Racquel sobbed.

"Hell no I won't take your crazy ass to my cousin's house so you can disrupt his life like you have done ours for the entire night."

"Well, can you at least tell me where it is and I'll find it on my own?"

"No. Now please leave us alone, Racquel," Lisa said as the tears began to flow down her face.

"How do you know Shawn is not in trouble, Mom?" Davonna interrupted.

"Call your cousin if you are feeling concerned," she responded.

"I'll do better then that. I'm going over there with Racquel."

"No, Davonna!" Racquel said while looking directly

at Lisa. "I don't know what is going on, and you have had enough traumas."

"I'm going with you. I will never be able to sleep again unless I get to the bottom of this whole thing. My fucking mother thinks I'm crazy, but I'm not — and I think you know that now, Racquel!" Davonna yelled while stomping into her room to get her sweater.

"Well, fuck it, then!" Lisa screamed, startling both Racquel and Davonna. "Let's all go. Give me five minutes to say a prayer and reload my pistol and I'll be ready."

While Lisa was in the back, Racquel dialed the number to her nephew, Detective Michael Mathews. She had no idea what to expect upon arriving at her destination. She would feel a lot safer with her nephew there. Besides the fact of his being a detective for the Columbus Police Department, Michael had always been very close with her. Not only was Racquel his favorite aunt, she was his only aunt and he was her only nephew. Michael was her only sister's son. Racquel and her sister Toya had gotten an apartment together around the time that Michael was two or three months old. During this time Racquel was in the beginning of her pregnancy with Felicia. The two sisters raised Michael and Felicia together until Michael was in the first grade. Both of the children's fathers were absent from their lives. Racquel maintained a simple life, working odd jobs and steadily searching for her soul mate. Toya was on the wilder side, jumping from man to man and falling

victim to sex, money, and drugs. Although the two children remained in the same neighborhood and continued
to be raised as brother and sister instead of cousins, their
lives as teenagers took two totally different paths. Michael
joined the YBE and got involved with all kinds of criminal
activities. Felicia, on the other hand, was a straight-A student and captain of the cheerleading team for Walnut Ridge
High school. She seemed to have a bright future ahead of
her. Things began to change for her once she gave her vir-
ginity to David. He was all that mattered from that point
on. Felicia's grades began to slip and she quit the cheerleading team in order to spend more time with David. Michael
would often warn her about associating with a man like
David. The two had done a lot of dirt together and he defi-
nitely did not approve of him being involved with his little
cousin. At one point Michael even confronted David about
his relationship with Felicia, warning him not to let any
harm come to her. David laughed off Michael's threats as
if they didn't need to be taken seriously. On the outside he
knew that Michael was just an overprotective big cousin.
On the inside David felt hatred and jealousy for Michael.
He did not appreciate any other man having feelings for
Felicia, cousin or not. Although he knew his jealousy was
completely uncalled-for, it still existed. There was nothing
he would like more than to take Michael into a field and
blow his brains ten feet away from his body. After the attack
on Michael and his mother, David was semi satisfied. He

married Felicia and forbade her to ever speak her cousin's name again. Felicia's love for her husband made her reluctantly obey the order, but this still did not satisfy David. The vigilante attacks and constant police harassments committed by Michael over the years only engraved David's hatred for him into his heart.

The phone rang three times before Detective Michael Mathews answered.

"Mathews speaking. Who is this?" he answered in an aggravated tone.

"It's your Aunt Racquel. Listen, baby, I need you to meet me somewhere. It's a matter of life and death."

"Where at, and what's wrong?" Michael asked in a concerned tone.

"I don't know exactly where yet, but I'll be there in a few minutes," Racquel said, realizing how crazy she must sound.

"Slow down, Auntie. You are not making any sense. Tell me what's going on," Michael responded while trying not to be noticed by the car he was trailing.

"Your cousin has been missing for days. I'm sure you know that all of your friends have been turning up dead."

"Her friends, Auntie, not mine," Michael said in an angry tone.

"This is no time to be technical, Michael," Racquel said in a stern tone. "Felicia is in some kind of trouble. She called me and said she was at old man Fletcher's brother

Shawn's house when the call got disconnected. I'm at his cousin Davonna's house now and she is going to take me over there. I really need you, Michael. I'll call you with the directions as soon as I find out where we are going."

The shock of what he just heard and what was taking place in front of his eyes made him drop the phone. The car he was trailing just turned down the street where the Hustler lived. As Michael slowly approached the corner of Seibert and Ann, he could still see the tail lights of the car that the two YBE members were in. Tony got out of the car and headed down the alley. Michael knew this routine all to well. Tony was going to case the house out while Daniel went inside to make the transaction. What startled him was the fact that they were going into the same house that his aunt was headed to.

"What the fuck is Felicia doing at the Hustler's house?" the detective asked himself. "Maybe she delivered the message to Tony and all of this is just a setup. But why did she call Aunt Racquel?"

Instead of going along with his original plan, the detective decided to just sit back and see how things unfolded, at least until his aunt arrived. Although Felicia and he did not see eye to eye, Michael still loved his only aunt and did not want anything to happen to her. He picked up the cell phone from off the floor of the car in hopes of finding the number that Racquel had called him from. To his disappointment, the number she dialed him from was private.

The only way to ensure his aunt's safety would be to head her off before she reached the house. But that would blow his cover and ruin his plan. He had no idea how soon they would be arriving or what kind of car she would be in. The only way for his plan to work without his aunt being hurt or seeing his evil side would be to act now. While thinking of a game plan, the detective exited his car and opened the trunk. He placed his bullet proof vest over his head and checked the many weapons he carried for rounds. He knew the first thing he had to do was take care of Tony, which was not going to be an easy task. There was no way of knowing what his state of mind was, or if Felicia had delivered the message he had given her. If this whole thing was a setup, then he could end up in the crossfire.

"Well, there's no time for second guesses now. Let's make this shit happen!" the detective said as he slowly crept down the alley that Tony had gone down a few minutes earlier.

Chapter 15

"What's the good word?" Daniel greeted as he walked through the Hustler's front door.

"You tell me, big baby! That damn H. Johnson's was closed. I figured you would rather meet here anyway," a voice came from the kitchen.

"You know them motherfuckers only open up when they want to. Why the hell are you sitting in the dark?" Daniel asked while placing his hand on his pistol and taking half a step to the left in order to get a better view of the kitchen.

"The goddamn fuse blew in the kitchen. Just push that door up behind you and have a seat. I'm getting you together right now."

Daniel's instincts were telling him that something was not right with this meeting. He pushed the door up and sat down on the love seat. His eyes were glued on the large figure in the kitchen that he thought to be the Hustler. The fact that the figure was motionless from the time he walked into the house heightened his suspicions.

"Hustler, are you all right in there?" Daniel hollered into the kitchen.

After getting no response, he pulled his Desert Eagle from his waistband and cocked it back as hard as he could in an attempt to change the mind of whatever plan the Hustler had. The whereabouts of his right-hand man were also running through his head. Daniel had no idea if Tony set this whole situation up or what his next move would be. The only thing he knew was that whatever was going on was about to unfold in a matter of seconds. While holding the Desert Eagle in both hands, he took dead aim on the Hustler's figure, which was still motionless, and inched his way toward the kitchen. As he took his second step, the remaining lights in the house went out.

Tony sat in the large apple tree behind the Hustler's house. His catlike abilities allowed him to climb the tree while carrying an AK 47 with no problems. His tree- climbing ability was a skill that followed him since the fifth grade. That's how his childhood friend turned detective knew exactly where to find him. Michael sat in the yard next door to the Hustler's house and carefully watched Tony in the tree. The clever detective was also in a position where he could see any cars pulling up in the front of the house. He was going to have to make his move now before Racquel showed up. He aimed his gun at Tony. There was no way he could miss from that position. His forehead began to sweat as he slowly placed his finger on the trigger.

"I got twenty dollars you miss," David said while placing his hand on the detective's shoulder.

Michael Mathews knew exactly who that voice belonged to. His heart pounded wildly inside his chest. He was certain that his mind was playing tricks on him, but there was no time to analyze his sanity. He swung around and pointed his pistol in the direction of the voice. To his surprise, there was no one there.

"What the fuck is going on?" he whispered to himself.

The rustle from the leaves alerted Tony. He quickly turned and pointed his weapon in the direction of the noise. At the same time he noticed the lights in the Hustler's house disappear from the corner of his eye. Although he wondered what was taking place inside of the house, it did not distract him from whatever was in the next yard. His instincts would not allow it. Tony sat as motionless as an owl in the center of the tree with his eyes and weapon focused in the direction of the noise. His target was identified as he watched Detective Mathews spinning in circles, waving his gun frantically. Michael's police experience, mixed with years of street knowledge, took over as he instinctively dove behind a pile of chopped wood and resumed his aim on the tree where Tony sat.

"What the hell are you two waiting for? Shoot, goddamit!" David whispered to himself while leaning against the house watching the standoff between his two enemies.

All three men's attention was broken by the sound of five shots being let off from inside the house. Tony knew that Michael came here for more than just him, and would be just as anxious to know what was going on inside the house. He took a deep breath and jumped out of the tree, hitting the ground hard while still holding on to the AK 47. As he rolled over and headed for the window at the rear of the house, he caught a glimpse of Michael hopping the fence and running to the side of the house while pointing his pistol in a standard police type of way. Although the agreement was not verbally confirmed, it would seem that the two had formed an alliance. At least until they both reached the inside of the house.

"OK, motherfuckers! You wanna play? I'll give all you bastards what the fuck y'all looking for!" Daniel yelled at the top of his lungs, trying to scare off whoever else was in the house.

Each of the five shots had hit the Hustler's large body. As Daniel watched the huge man slowly fall over, his heart pounded even faster. The man did not make a sound after taking five hits. His body fell the exact way it was sitting. As he finally reached the kitchen, Daniel looked down at the Hustler's bloody, bullet- riddled body. He noticed that his hands were tied and his mouth was duct-taped. Now he was sure this was a setup. The Hustler telling him to close the door and have a seat replayed in his mind. How could he have been talking if his mouth was taped? Getting out of the house took over any other thoughts in Daniel's mind. As he turned around in an attempt to head for the door, Felicia slapped him viciously with a cast iron skillet. He hit the floor hard and fought even harder to remain conscious. His Desert Eagle slid across the floor and hit David's foot.

"Ain't no fun when the rabbit got the gun, huh?" David said with a grin, bending down to pick up the weapon. "I want you to get a good look at me! Look at me, you motherfucker!"

David's face was bloody, beaten, and burned just as it was the night of his death. Felicia looked at her husband with no fear or emotion. She was sure that her soul was going to hell and David was the demon that was going to carry it there. Her mind was completely gone and her body was willing to accept her fate. The only functions left in her body were controlled by David. Tony watched the events from the back window while Michael witnessed the situation from the side window. Neither could believe their eyes, but both were too scared to move. Tony was confused about where his loyalty should be. Should he try to rescue Felicia and Daniel from the demon, or should he let his best friend get his revenge? Michael was equally confused about his next move. He somehow knew all along that David was behind all of the city's recent murders. The question was did he fake his death, or was this some sort of gangsta-like zombie? The fact that his cousin was still obsessed with this punk and willing to become his servant of evil made the detective hate Felicia even more. He continued to watch in horror as David picked Daniel up with one hand and threw him across the kitchen. The idea of David faking his death had disappeared now. The beating Daniel was receiving had to be fueled by an unrested soul.

"Wait! Wait! Please, I can pay you. Whatever you want, just let me go!" Daniel begged, attempting to crawl under the kitchen table.

"Does it look like I would have any use for your god-damn money now? You took my life from me, in my own home, in front of my woman. You violated the rules of the game by involving her. If you had an issue with me, you should have confronted me like a man. Instead you and your faggot ass peons sneaked into my house like a bunch of cowards and murdered me. Well, now it's your turn, boss."

"Tony, where the hell are you?" Daniel yelled as loud as he could.

"His punk ass is hiding under the window over there," David responded while pointing to the window. "It seems as if he's not too good at saving people. Where was he when you and your crew were beating the hell out of me and my naked wife?"

Tony sat under the window holding his gun, completely terrified. David knew he was there and probably had plans for him after he was finished with Daniel. Maybe with the help of the detective and Daniel, they could take David down and save Felicia. Knowing that this would be the battle of his life, he took a deep breath and prayed that the detective would follow his lead. Against his better judgment, Tony walked over to the patio doors, shot out the glass, and entered the kitchen to face his former best friend. He had never feared anything breathing before in his life. The fact that David stopped breathing a while ago scared the hell out of Tony.

The detective watched in disbelief as Tony entered the scene.

"That fool must have lost his damn mind," Michael whispered to himself. "He can't be that loyal to Daniel."

With a nod of his head, David instructed Felicia to attack Tony. Screaming at the top of her lungs, she ran across the room swinging the skillet. David flipped over the kitchen table and slapped Daniel across the head with the Desert Eagle. Tony was trying desperately to fight off Felicia without hurting her. Although she weighed a little more than half of what Tony did, she was putting up a hell of a fight.

"What's wrong, bra? Is the little lady being rude?" David looked over at Tony and said with a half of a grin on his face, "Felicia, don't be rude. Tony is one of our closest friends. It would be dead wrong to make him suffer for what old punk ass Daniel did to us. Remember, he did try to save us, so please, kill him quickly."

As soon as the words left the demon's mouth Felicia seemed to grow twice as strong. She threw her opponent to the ground as if he were a five-year-old instead of a grown man. Unlike his so-called boss, Tony held on to his gun and pointed it at the monstrous couple while crawling over to

Daniel. Felicia withdrew her weapon at the same time and pointed it at both men. Seeing his little cousin with a gun pointed at her made the detective go into a rage. Although the two no longer saw eye to eye, he had protected her since childhood and still felt a slight obligation to do so. Their past and her dead husband were instantly forgotten as he ran through the front door with his weapon drawn.

"Drop that fucking gun, Tony!" Michael yelled while pointing his gun at the two men on the floor.

"What the fuck is your silly ass doing, Mike? Does it look like they need any more help?" Daniel yelled in a frustrated voice.

"Actually we never needed your help, Mr. Policeman!" David said as he slammed the front door and smiled at the detective. "My day seems to be getting better and better by the minute. I was wondering how long you were going to sit on the side of the house without joining our little party. You know this thing just would not be right without our friendly neighborhood cop. I can't tell you how good it is to see us all reunited again. But like all good things, it's about time for this party to end."

"Fuck all of you motherfuckers. My cousin and I are getting the hell out of here. You three can sit here and play with each other all night if you want to."

The detective's actions slowly began to break down the trance that Felicia was in. She really did not know who to trust now. The detective had just threatened to pin his partner's murder on her a few days ago; now he was trying to save her. Tony's loyalty to her was never in question, but David wanted him dead and here lately David got what he wanted.

"Felicia, please put the gun down," Tony begged. "I don't want to hurt you."

"Then you drop your gun, motherfucker!" the detective yelled.

"I've told you more than once that Felicia is my woman now and she doesn't need your help, cousin!" David yelled with extreme rage while grabbing the man by the neck and lifting him into the air.

"No, baby — please! Let him live. We can kill everyone else, but please let my family live," Felicia begged while turning her attention away from the two men lying on the floor.

Tony and Daniel saw this as their chance to get away. Daniel ran toward the patio door as Tony followed closely behind pointing his weapon. Before the two could escape, David appeared at the patio doorway with the detective still in hand. Tony fired a shot directly into David's face.

"You know, this situation is really putting a strain on our friendship, Tony," David said as he slapped the gun from his hand.

Daniel grabbed a large butcher knife off the counter and rushed at David. With inhuman speed and strength, David threw the detective on Daniel.

"I'm tired of playing now. Felicia, kill all three of these bastards," the demon ordered with fire in his eyes.

"Not Michael."

"What did you just say?"

"I said I'm not killing my own cousin, David. I don't care what you do to me."

The car containing Racquel, Bubba, Lisa, and Davonna was pulling up at the same time. Although Racquel and Lisa were fairly large women, they both managed to hop out of the car almost before it stopped moving. Davonna and Bubba were close behind.

"I'm warning you not to disobey me, baby. Now kill these motherfuckers so this shit can be over with," David demanded.

"No! You kill them if you want them dead. From here on out you can commit your own murders."

"You know what, baby? I think you're right. It's time for me to get my own hands dirty."

As Racquel attempted to knock on the Hustler's door it swung open and there stood David. Before she could say a word, he twisted her head completely to the back of her. Davonna screamed to the top of her lungs at the sight of David. With all of the speed and strength that Bubba could build up, he rushed at the image that had just murdered his lady. David swatted the man away as if he were a huge insect. Felicia fell on top of her mother's lifeless body as David proceeded to attack and dominate all four men with ease. Lisa stood at the front door in complete amazement. She raised her weapon and emptied it into the kitchen without caring who she hit. Four of her six shots hit David in the back while the other two struck Tony in the shoulder. As Daniel made another attempt for the patio door, David grabbed him by the back of the neck. With brute force he rammed his head into Bubba's head, knocking both men out cold. The detective lay in the corner playing dead, hoping the demon would overlook him. It was the only plan of surviving this nightmare his frightened soul could come up with. After seeing that bullets had no effect on the creature, Lisa was convinced that this was a fight she wanted nothing to do with.

"Run, baby!" Lisa instructed Davonna, backing away from the door.

"That might be kinda hard for her to do right about now," David said in a sarcastic tone.

As Lisa turned in her daughter's direction she saw David holding Davonna's bloody, lifeless body in his arms with her insides torn completely out. Anger instantly took over her fear as she lunged at the creature.

"Didn't you see what happened when Bubba's big ass just tried that? You people are really starting to piss me off. Play time is over!"

David grabbed Lisa by the top of her hair and dragged the woman screaming and kicking back toward the house. Michael had just crawled over to Racquel's body and put his arms around Felicia.

"Come on, cuz. We got to get the hell outta here before he comes back."

"I'm already back!" David said in the same horrific voice that shook the entire house.

Lisa could not say a word as her large body was lifted into the air. She felt the pressure of David's cold, clammy palms on both sides of her face. Lisa's last thoughts splattered all over Felicia and Michael as her head was crushed between David's hands like a huge grape. The detective's heart was pumping faster than it ever had before. He wanted to run, but knew there was no way for him to escape. Felicia seemed to not be bothered by the events taking place around her. She gently wiped the brain matter that had fallen from Lisa's body off of her mother's face.

"Mom! Please wake up, Mom. I'm so sorry. David didn't mean it. Tell her that you didn't mean it, baby," Felicia begged.

"Mom knows that I love her. Now, baby, will you please get up so we can finish this? I had no intention of turning this into an all-night event. I done missed the last match on wrestling and everything."

"We have to get Mom to a hospital!"

"It's too late for that, baby. Your mother is dead. Everybody is dead except for the people that I came all the way back from hell to kill! Now if you love me like you say you do then I suggest you get up right now and kill the rest of these bastards."

As usual, the challenge of her love for David was all the inspiration that Felicia needed. She looked over at her cousin with the same fire in her eyes that her husband had. The detective knew that he was in trouble. His eyes searched the room frantically for his weapon, but could find only the one in his cousin's hand. Before he could react, Felicia fired a shot into his arm.

"I guess I'll leave you two alone. It seems like y'all have some family issues to discuss," David said sarcastically as he entered the kitchen.

As the demon walked past Bubba he raised his foot high into the air and brought it down on the back of the man's neck, breaking it instantly. Ignoring the pain from the two bullets that hit him earlier, Tony grabbed his gun off the floor and stood to face his former best friend.

"I know what you want, David. You always wanted me to choose between you and Daniel. If I make the choice will that put an end to all of this?" Tony asked while lifting Daniel to his feet and placing the gun to the back of his head.

"Why is everyone on the damn monster's side tonight?" Daniel yelled.

"Shut up, motherfucker! You caused all of this," Tony yelled while shoving the barrel of his pistol into the man's head harder.

"Baby! Come in here and bring ol' super cop with you.

I want everybody to see this. It seems Tony has a gift for us. He's decided to stop being a puppet for the great leader of the YBE and kill his boss, just for us. I probably would have appreciated it a little more if you could have managed to kill him before he killed me, but better late then never."

With great strength, Felicia dug her two middle fingers into Michael's bullet wound and dragged him into the kitchen. While standing next to her husband, a bloody mess, she could actually see past the evil in his face and notice a look of satisfaction. She looked over at Tony and felt a sense of gratitude for once again having her husband's back. Everything was going to be all right now, as far as she was concerned. David had his revenge, and she had proven her love to him. Once Tony killed Daniel and she killed her cousin, everything would be all right. With a smile on her face she looked into David's eyes and said, "I love you."

"Stop and think about what you are doing, Tony," Daniel begged.

"I know what has to be done. It is the only way David can rest."

As fast as he could, Tony pointed his weapon and fired. The bullet struck Felicia directly in the forehead. The entire room was silent as the life slowly drained out of Felicia's body. Upon seeing his wife hit the floor, David released a yell that could be heard for blocks. His burnt skin slowly began to fall off of his face. The rest of his body seemed to liquefy and within seconds he was nothing more than a puddle of blood and pus on the floor. Daniel and Michael both stared at Tony with a look of disbelief.

"How did you know that killing Felicia would destroy David?" the detective asked, trying to catch his breath.

"He was my best friend. I know him like the back of my hand. Dead or alive there was no way he would send Felicia through all of this unless he really needed her. I once heard them say that they breathed for each other. They lived for each other. She was his better half, and as long as one lived the other would also exist. The love they had for each other allowed his soul to return."

"Whatever! Fuck him and that crazy bitch. If I had known all this shit was going to happen, I would have shot her right along with that motherfucker!" Daniel said, rubbing the back of his head.

Tony and Michael both looked at each other and seemed to have the same thoughts. Without warning, both men emptied their weapons into Daniel's chest. As the leader of the YBE fell to the ground, the detective walked over and spat in his face.

"That's for my mother, you son of a bitch!"

Tony dropped his weapon and headed for the door. The blood and bodies that were splattered all over the house had begun to take on a ripe smell. Although Michael was in an enormous amount of pain, his mind was still going a hundred miles a minute. He had to figure out a way to explain all of the night's events and the number of dead, mutilated bodies. He thought it might be a good idea if Tony and he got their story straight. He called out to Tony while bending over to pick up Felicia's gun.

"What are we gonna say about tonight?"

"I'm not gonna say shit. You are the detective. Come up with something. I'm going home, fix my damn shoulder, and try my best to forget this night ever happened."

"So I guess you are the new leader of the YBE now?"

"Fuck the YBE — I'm done!"

"You know my beef never really was with you," the detective said, extending his hand in an attempt to call a truce.

Tony turned around and shook his former friend's hand. As he did, the detective placed Felicia's weapon under Tony's chin and fired, blowing the top of his head into the air. After quickly searching for a rag, he wiped his prints off of the weapon and placed it in Tony's hand. Looking out the open front door, he noticed the green DeVille parked in the driveway and remembered the large duffel bag that Daniel was carrying earlier. With bag in hand, the detective fled the scene.

After leaving the hospital, Michael filled out his report saying that he arrived at the scene and was shot by Tony who then killed himself. The case was ruled as murder/suicide. The other murders that had recently taken place were also pinned on Tony and their cases closed due to the murder weapon being found in his possession.

Chapter 16

There was barely room to park at the funeral home on Hudson and Hamilton. The people there were worn out from the enormous amounts of funerals that they had attended in the past week. The city of Columbus seemed to be in a gloomy state due to all of the massacres that had recently taken place. It would seem as if an entire generation had been wiped out. The mothers of all the victims glanced at each other with evil eyes as if each blamed the other's child. Felicia lay in her casket awaiting her journey to hell. She was completely surprised at the turnout of her funeral, considering her past actions. She could hear what sounded like hundreds of voices. She wished she could see what was going on, but the hole in her head called for a closed casket. That was the least of her worries. Whatever hell had in store for her was her main concern. As the preacher began to talk she replayed all of the past events of her life. The neighborhood she grew up in and all of her associates. Being popular herself and then dating a member of the most feared group in Columbus. Her wedding day was the most joyous day of her life. Her mom was so happy for her. The fact that her baby would be married before she had any children gave Racquel great joy. As a matter of fact, all of Felicia's accomplishments gave Racquel a greater joy than anything else in life. Felicia could not remember a time where her mother did not make her feel as if the sun rose and set because of her, and now she was dead. She remembered how nervous she was on the day of her wedding and how Davonna was right there with her through the whole thing. The two were best friends through pimples, puberty, and periods, and now she was dead. She remembered how hurt Michael was about his mom becoming a crack head and how disappointed he was with her for marrying David. She thought about the man that she loved so dearly and how he was the reason for almost all of these situations. She had allowed this man to take her on a path of destruction. Even after he was dead. For some strange reason it did not make her love him any less. In a strange way she was happy that at least now he could rest. Knowing that even after all of the pain she felt and caused, she probably would do the same again was what convinced her that she deserved to be in hell. She wanted to cry, but assumed that her tears would be replaced by embalming fluid. Her thoughts were interrupted by her casket being lifted by the pallbearers. The ride to the cemetery was shorter than she wanted it to be. After a few more words from the preacher she could feel her casket being lowered into the ground. After what seemed to be hours she could hear the dirt hitting the roof of the casket as her grave was being filled. It took no time at all for the earthly insects to make their way into the casket and crawl all over her. They entered every opening of her body, including the bullet hole in her forehead. Felicia's extreme fear of bugs reassured her that hell must be her sentence and there would be no chance of heaven for her. She began to hear a faint but familiar voice. Fearing it might be the devil, she tried to ignore it. The more she tried, the louder it became.

"Baby! Wake up, baby."

It can't be, she thought.

"Wake up, baby. We are not finished yet. We have a lot more work to do. I still need you."

"Please, David, let me rest. Haven't you done enough?"

"If you love me, then you will wake up!"

As usual, that was all the encouragement she needed. Felicia opened her eyes and ran her fist straight through the roof of the casket.